KITTY
SLADE

Raven Hearts

fiona dunbar

ORCHARD

ORCHARD BOOKS
338 Euston Road, London NW1 3BH
Orchard Books Australia
Level 17/207 Kent Street, Sydney, NSW 2000

First published in the UK in 2012 by Orchard Books

ISBN 978 1 40830 931 5

Text © Fiona Dunbar 2012

The right of Fiona Dunbar to be identified as the author of this work has been
asserted by her in accordance with the Copyright, Designs and Patents Act, 1988.

A CIP catalogue record for this book is available from the British Library.

1 3 5 7 9 10 8 6 4 2

Printed in Great Britain

Orchard Books is a division of Hachette Children's Books,
an Hachette UK company.

www.hachette.co.uk

For Stuart, Jo-Anne, Gabby and Ross

Archie Booth

DVDs.

That's what you need, and plenty of them, if you're going to survive the hell that is the entire length of the M3 motorway, plus most of the M1, plus sizeable chunks of other, more rubbish roads. In a hulking great Hippo of a camper van that only ever reaches about fifty-five miles an hour.

Oh, and don't let your brother be in charge of DVD selection. Trust me: I speak from experience. Somehow I didn't get to be around when the Big Road Trip DVD collection was put together, so while there *was* stuff I liked from way back, none of my recent faves were there. No vampires, no rom-coms. Flossie seemed to have snuck some of hers in, I noticed, but she was the *only* one who liked *High School Musical*.

The Big Road Trip, incidentally, was basically our life

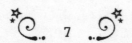

now. The Hippo was our home, Maro (our grandmother) was our driver and teacher, and we were free to go where we wanted. No fixed abode, no school. Great, huh? Well…yes and no.

Sam pulled out a Harry Potter film.

'Yay!' said Flossie.

I groaned. 'You know what? I'm not in the mood.'

'Kitty! Not in the mood? How can you not be in the mood for Harry Potter?' said Sam.

I sighed. 'Too many ghosts.'

'Uh?' protested Flossie. 'But there's also wizards and magic, and–'

'And ghosts,' I said. 'Look, I get enough of that stuff in real life; I could use a break, OK?'

Flossie folded her arms tightly. 'Not fair!'

Ha! Not fair? Was it fair on *me* that I was stuck seeing dead people all over the place, whether I liked it or not? But no way was Flossie ever going to understand that, not in a million years…

'Come on,' I said, gesturing to Sam. 'There must be something else.'

Nothing seemed to fit the bill. Finally, Sam said, 'OK: is creepy allowed, as long as there's no ghosts?'

'We-ell…'

'Come on; you'll be fine with this,' he said, pulling

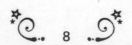

out his Alfred Hitchcock collection. Sam's a total Alfred Hitchcock geek. I secretly don't mind some of those movies, but I so wouldn't tell him that; he'd never shut up about it. Seriously.

Flossie groaned loudly. 'Oh, not *old* movies.'

'Just go with it,' insisted Sam, putting on a film called *The Birds*.

'Is it black-and-white?' asked Flossie.

'No.'

'Oh, all right.'

The Birds is about this woman who gets attacked by a seagull out on some remote island; next thing you know, she's convalescing, then hanging out full-time… Anyway, soon it starts getting weird, and the birds start ganging up on the humans, whole flocks of them. Then they're attacking people all over the place, and nobody knows why. The end gets cheesy though, because that's when the special effects come in. Fail! Well, it was made in 1963. That's not just pre-CGI, that's pre-just-about-everything. Sam wasn't pleased when me and Flossie just laughed.

'Oh you kids, you're so hard to please,' Maro called back from the driving seat. 'I remember being scared stiff of that film!'

'The trouble with *them* is, they can't use their imaginations,' said Sam.

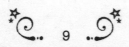

'Sam?' I said.

'Yeah?'

'Stop being a pompous ar—'

'Language!' snapped Maro.

'Why d'you s'pose they made it about birds,' said Flossie, 'and not, like, swarms of bees or something?'

'Because that *would* be cheesy,' said Sam.

'Plus, I've got to admit, birds are kind of creepy,' I said.

'Well, you know, in art, they symbolise departed souls,' said Maro.

'What, you mean, like, ghosts?' said Flossie.

'Yes: ghosts, spirits.'

'So was that a ghost story then?'

'No, of course not,' said Sam. 'It's about *birds*.'

'How do you know they're not *symbolising* dead people?' I said. 'Use your imagination, *Sam*.'

He made a rude gesture at me.

After that I zizzed off, and dreamt I was being pursued by a gang of massive human-sized crows – which, trust me, was a hell of a lot scarier and less silly than it sounds. So much for not watching anything spooky. I needed to get Maro down to the shops pdq next time we were in a town, and pick some movies *I* wanted.

*

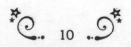

'Why are people staring at us?' I asked, as we rumbled over towards our pitch at the caravan park. So far we'd mostly been parking the Hippo in people's driveways and stuff. But here in Yorkshire, where we were staying for a while on our way up to Scotland, we didn't really know anybody. Which is why we wound up here at the Adlington Beck Caravan Park, being stared at.

'They're just curious,' said Maro.

'Nosy, more like,' said Sam.

'Staring is rude,' said Flossie.

'It's just human nature,' said Maro. 'You'd be curious, too. Anyway, you want people to be interested, don't you? Maybe we'll make some new friends.'

I stared out at the grey-haired couple in the zip-up cardies who were tending this completely OTT rockery garden they had beside their caravan, crammed with statuettes. 'Uh-huh…*right*.'

'Of course there may not be any kids here, it being term-time,' said Maro, cheerfully. 'But that needn't matter!'

'*Ri-i-ight*,' I said.

Hadn't thought of that. Now it finally dawned on me that not only would kids not be around during school hours; they just wouldn't be here, period. Because families don't hang out at caravan parks unless they're on holiday, and of course they don't take holidays

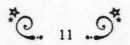

during term-time. Urgh. This was going to be so dull. What was more, it looked like any minute it was going to pelt down with rain.

A man came over and guided us to our pitch. 'I'll go and fetch Brian for yer,' he said, and disappeared. Maro parked on the pitch, with all the usual faffing that entails. Lurching back and forth, back and forth, crunching gears, stalling. Embarrassing. I could just *feel* all those people staring, thinking, *Who's this idiot?*

And what was the first thing I saw when we got out? A ruddy great scary black bird, perched on the fence opposite. I froze. 'Whoah!'

'Oh look,' said Maro. 'A raven!'

Sam was delighted. 'Whoo, creepy!' he said. 'Next thing you know, they'll all be lining up along here, and–'

'Yeah, yeah,' I said. The raven cocked its head to one side and stared at me with its little black beady eye. 'For God's sake, even the *birds* stare at you round here! What is it with this place?'

'Shh!' hissed Sam. 'Don't be so rude!'

I looked around. 'Chill out! Nobody heard. It's just...' I looked at the raven again. Still, it held its gaze. 'Yeah, it's creepy.'

The raven cocked its head the other way, cawed loudly, then flapped away.

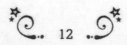

'It's just a harmless bird, *Kitaki-mou,*' said Maro. 'It's not going to attack you or anything.' She staggered out into the clearing beside the pitch and started doing these weird stretches. 'Ooh…ooh…ah!'

'What are you *doing*?' I asked.

'Ooh…long drive, sweetie, long drive…aah, my joints!' She doubled over, clasped her hands behind her and swung them up in the air. 'Oh, hello!' she said from between her legs, blood collected in her raspberry-coloured upside-down face, white hair dangling.

I looked over to see a tall man standing nearby, holding a clipboard. Brian, no doubt. 'Mrs…Slade?' he said, peering sideways at her.

Me, Sam and Floss all looked at each other, cringing with embarrassment.

'Ooh, ah! Yes!' said Maro, straightening herself out, and losing her balance in the process.

Brian stepped forward and reached out to steady her. 'Ha ha ha, there you go…all right?'

Maro was hooting with laughter at this point, and swearing in Greek. '*Oh, po po, ti messi mou,* my aching back!'

Mr and Mrs Zip-up Cardie stood there with their secateurs, staring. The cupid statuette stared. Nearby, a large ceramic frog stared, bug-eyed. Several of our

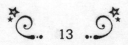

13

other new neighbours were staring, too.

'I'm Brian,' said the man, 'we spoke on the phone.'

We spork on the phorn. I'd have to get used to this accent.

'Ah yes,' said Maro. She introduced us, then gazed around. 'What a lovely place you have here; charming. And the view! Look, kids! Vista!'

Like we hadn't noticed already. It *was* a lovely spot; lush green hills in every direction, dotted with sheep and bordered with the same craggy dry-stone walls we'd been seeing all over the place.

'So that's Ilkley Moor?' said Maro, gesturing to the hills.

'No, that's all farmland you see there,' said Brian. 'The moor's just out that way, to the south. Have you not been here before?'

'No, never.'

'Ah, it's one of the loveliest parts of the country, this,' said Brian, proudly. 'Beautiful...mysterious... a wilderness. "Solid rock deeper than any sea": Ted Hughes.' He paused for us to be all impressed. 'Like all beautiful things, it's also deadly,' he added gravely.

'It is? They are?' said Maro.

Brian suddenly lightened up. 'Oh, only if you don't take proper precautions! You'd be amazed at some

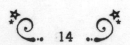

people. So I always warn newcomers, like. If you're heading right into the heart of the moor, you take a good map, and provisions, you check the forecast…all common sense, really.'

'Oh, don't worry…we're sensible, aren't we, kids?' said Maro.

'Oh, *dead* sensible,' I said.

The next day, I met some of those dead *non*-sensible types.

Uninspiring though the caravan park was, we had at least wanted to go for a wander round it – but then it had begun to pour with rain. So having already been stuck in the Hippo for most of the day, we were cooped up again with frozen pizza and the telly. Even the campsite's broadband wasn't working, which totally sucked.

By the next morning, we were all *desperate* to get out, so we caught a bus to the moor.

Flossie wasn't inspired. She sat slumped next to me on the bus. 'I think the moor sounds *boring*,' she moaned. 'I mean, what *is* a moor? It's just grass, isn't it? Big old load of grass. Nothing fun in it. Boring.'

'Flossie!' said Sam. 'There's much more than that! Didn't you read your info sheets?'

'Oh that, yeah,' said Flossie. 'I forgot: there's rocks too. Rocks an' grass.'

Maro chuckled. 'Just you wait, *pethaki-mou*. It's a bit more interesting than you make it sound–'

'*Moor* interesting, geddit?' said Sam poking Flossie from behind. '*Moor* interesting!'

I rolled my eyes. 'Yup, got it, Sam.'

Maro, oblivious, was meanwhile rabbiting on about all the errands and stuff she had to do. '...So today's just a short walk anyway. Ah, look, we're right on the edge of it now. See?'

Flossie looked unimpressed. 'And ferns. Lots of ferns.'

When we got off the bus, we were way up high, with wide-open space in every direction. Flossie became mildly more interested as we got closer to some rocks which, it soon became clear, were actually these whacking great cliffs. One part had a big hunk of rock leaning out from it, and there was another, smaller one like it that had fallen down at some point. These were called the Cow and Calf. Climbing the path towards the cliffs, you could see there was an opening, and the path led right through the gap. Flossie, now totally excited, ran up and into the opening. We all followed, and found ourselves surrounded on three sides by these massive

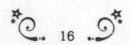

rock crags, high as office blocks.

'Whoah!' said Sam.

'This is sooo cool!' said Flossie.

'Yup: haunted, too,' I said, gazing around at the several misshapen ghosts that were moping about the place.

'Yeah?'

'Uh-huh.'

'Says here, it's a very popular place for rock climbers,' said Maro, reading from her guidebook.

'Yeah, that figures,' I said. 'I guess some of them didn't actually know what the hell they were doing, so then...splat.'

We went back out and headed to the top the safe way. There were two paths: the easy one – gently sloping, winding around the hill – and the steep one, which was shorter and more direct, but also more challenging. Floss kept Maro company going round the long way, while Sam and I scrambled up the rocky path. Sam, annoyingly, got to the top way before me. Well, I had a shoelace issue. I'm actually a really good climber.

Anyway, the point is, by the time I got to the top, I was on my own for a bit. I gazed down into the massive rocky well, then felt giddy, so I stepped back. Then suddenly I felt this huge WHOOSH of cold air, and there in front of me stood a woman in a turquoise coat.

She came right up to me and grabbed my arm with her ice-cold hand. Intense gaze, deep-set eyes a bit too close together. Quite old, maybe seventy-something. She wore one of those headscarves they used to wear in the 1960s. Powdery face, red lipstick. Looked like an extra out of *The Birds*, actually. Said she was looking for her boy, Archie Booth. 'Have you seen him?' she asked.

Typical ghost; looking for some other dead person. Grandson, I supposed.

I glanced at the ghosts down below, thinking, surely he couldn't be one of them? She must have been able to see them herself. 'What does he look like?' I asked.

'Oh, he's a strapping lad, is our Archie,' she said. 'He…he loves his puds. I mean, he *did*, before… Oooh!' She chewed the knuckles of her gloved hand, then dabbed at her eyes with a hanky and sniffed. 'He's a little on the heavy side, I suppose. Last seen out here, on t' moor. And I'm that worried he'll perish, poor baby!' And then she really went off on one, wailing her heart out.

Blimey, I thought. *How to break it to her?*

Well, I figured I'd just go along with it, act as if there

was something I could do. 'Who was he with at the time?' I asked.

'Oh, he wasn't *with* anybody; he was alone.'

'*Alone?* But—'

'I know, I know…I've gone over and over it in my mind, wishing, wishing…'

The kid's mother must have been really neglectful, I thought. All the same, people don't usually just disappear into thin air. I cleared my throat. 'Well, um…did…I mean, *does* he like rock climbing?'

She shook her head. 'Oh no, he'd never do that.'

'OK…' I gazed down at the ghosts below; not a single one was overweight. Which didn't mean Archie couldn't have had an accident somewhere on the moor, of course – only you'd think he'd have been found, in that case.

Then the woman started to fade. 'Please: you must help me find him…please!'

'Well, I'll…I'll try.'

Again she grabbed my arm in her icy grip. 'You promise, now?' Man, she was intense!

'Look, I…' I sighed. 'OK, what was he wearing?'

'He was dressed warmly, at least.' She sniffed loudly. 'Yes, with his donkey jacket, his warm socks, his Doc Martens…they'd keep the worst of the cold out.' She

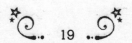

seemed desperate to find that reassuring…it was quite pathetic, really.

Now her spirit energy was waning; she faded some more.

'And…how old was…*is* he?' I asked, hurriedly.

But by now she had faded completely, so that was that.

The Raven

There didn't seem to be much in the way of ghosts at the campsite. I mean, plenty of people who seemed *half* dead, but not ones that were actually dead.

Later that day, we went for a wander, to see if there was *anyone* interesting there at all. We avoided the bit where Mr and Mrs Zip-up Cardie lived – the stationary-trailer part. Everyone there was old, and apparently only interested in keeping their cars shiny, and their gardens neat. Gardens the size of postage stamps but crammed with statuettes and furnished so they could sit out there like they were Lord of the Manor or something.

We headed down the other end, and wow: big contrast! Beat-up old cars, rusting gas canisters, piles of junk. We passed a man sitting outside his van. He wore tracky bottoms and trainers on his bottom half, and nothing on his big-bellied top half except half a dozen

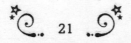

tattoos and a few gold chains. He was swigging from a can of beer, and attached to a lead tied to his chair was one of those dogs that permanently looks as if it's ready to eat your face off. All muscle and sinew and slobbering jaws. The dog barked at us, and the man barked at the dog. 'Carlos! Shut it!'

We hurried along, and turned back to where the other camper vans were. One of them really caught my eye; an old-fashioned green VW with 'Zoe' painted above the windscreen. It had ropes of beads hanging from the rear-view mirror, and a bunch of knick-knacks on the dash; buddhas and fake flowers and stuff. A young man in bare feet and purple trousers appeared beside it.

'Hey, hippiemobile!' laughed Sam. 'Wow, I can smell the incense from here.'

'Shh! He'll hear.'

'Who'll hear?'

'Him. The one with the…oh, hang on. You don't see him with the bare feet?'

'Nope.'

'Flossie?'

Flossie peered. 'Uh-uh. Must be a ghost, Kitty.'

'Oh, right. Hi!' I called, waving to the ghost. He smiled and waved back. 'Aah, sweet!' I said.

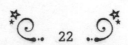

'Kitty!' hissed Sam. 'You want people to think you're crazy?'

I sighed. 'You know what? I'm tired of covering up my phantorama! So what if I see ghosts? I don't care who knows.'

After a moment, Flossie said, 'I suppose if *I* was seeing ghosts all the time, and *I* had to keep pretending I wasn't…I'd get pretty tired of that.'

I wrapped my arm around her and kissed her on the head. 'Thank you!'

Flossie smiled. 'You're welcome.'

'See?' I said to Sam. 'Flossie understands.'

'All right, I get it, no problem,' said Sam. 'Phantorama's general knowledge from now on.'

'Well, not *general* knowledge exactly, just…'

'Kitty, come on,' said Sam. 'Either it is or it isn't.'

'Look, all I know is, I'm fed up of pretending,' I said. 'Plus, you can't always tell the live people from the dead ones anyway. They're not *all* in big fat skirts and wigs, you know; don't *all* carry their heads around with them. Some of them are just like you and me–'

'Oh my God!' said Sam.

'What?'

'Look,' he said, pointing. 'A kid!'

There *was* a kid: a boy. Skinny and brown-skinned,

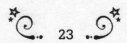

...lessly kicking a ball around. He stopped as we came ...ar, squinting at us from under his thick dark fringe.

'Hi,' said Sam.

'Hi.'

'I'm Sam; this is Kitty and Flossie. We just got here.'

The boy nodded. "Ow come you're not in school?'

Ow coom. He was a local. Although I guessed his family originated from somewhere much further away, like India.

'We're home-schooled,' I said. 'By our gran. We live in the camper van full-time now.'

The boy raised his eyebrows. 'And your mum an' dad?'

'Oh, mum died when we were very young,' I said. 'We never knew our dad. How come *you're* not in school?'

'Waiting for a place, like. Won't be one till September, probably. We're waiting for a home, an' all. Caravan's me uncle's.'

'So you're on your own all day?' asked Flossie.

'Well, me mum's here…and me sister,' said the boy. 'But she's only eighteen months. 'Ow long you here for, then?'

'Two, three weeks,' I said. 'So are there like, *no* other kids here at all?'

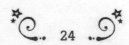

'Only on weekends,' said the boy. ''Side from that, everyone's in school, 'cept me.'

'Bummer,' said Sam.

The boy shrugged. ''S'all right. Better'n before, in me old school.'

'Why's that?' I asked.

'It were rubbish there; teachers shouting the whole time…me dad says I weren't learning owt anyway, might as well move to a different catchment area, get into a better school. Did you *ever* go to school?'

'Oh yeah,' said Sam. 'But…'

'We had to move out of our flat in London,' said Flossie.

'Well, it was a whole bunch of things, really,' Sam added vaguely, trailing off.

'I got booted out of school, 'cause of my phantorama,' I said at last.

The boy squinted at me. 'Because of your what?'

I shrugged. 'I see ghosts.'

'Oh.'

I was surprised at how underwhelmed he was.

'Did you hear what she said?' asked Flossie. 'She *sees ghosts*. And talks to them!'

'Ye-e-eah…' said the boy. He cleared his throat. 'See,

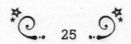

the thing is, you're talking about like, spirits of dead people, right?'

I squinted at him. 'Er, you know of any other kind?'

'Well, yeah, actually, I do,' said the boy.

Just then a squat lady in a sari appeared in the doorway of his caravan and yelled at him in a stream of complicated-sounding Urdu or whatever.

The boy complained, gesturing to us.

The lady looked at us, nodded, then apparently relented.

The boy ran up and gave her a big kiss; she laughed and babbled something else and went inside.

The boy came back to join us. 'I haven't got long; got to look after me sister. Hey, you want to go down by the stream?'

'Uh...OK, I guess.'

'I'm Kamal, by the way.'

We all introduced ourselves.

'So what other kind of ghosts are there then, besides the dead-person kind?' I asked him.

'Well, it's not like I seriously believe in them either,' he said, as he led us down past all the caravans to a dirt path that led into a wooded area. 'But, you know, there's all the stories about the jinn. A jinni is—'

'A genie?' I said.

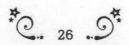

'No: *jinni*. J-I-N-N-I. But yeah, it's where the word "genie" comes from. Anyway, a jinni is not the spirit of a dead person, like the sort you're talking about, but a separate being.'

'A separate being?' I said. 'How? What?'

'Humans were created out of clay, and the jinn from smokeless fire, see? They're all around, like, but we don't see them.'

'Unless you have phantorama,' said Flossie.

'No, it's not these *jinn* I see, Floss: it's *ghosts*,' I said. I really was starting to feel quite confused.

'So, what happens, exactly, with the ghosts?' said Kamal. 'Do they, like…talk to you?'

'Well, sometimes,' I said.

By now we'd got down to the stream; it was a nice, peaceful spot, and completely deserted. 'So they know you can see and hear them, then,' said Kamal.

'Yes.'

Sam and Floss already knew I'd seen someone on the moor – I'd mentioned it briefly, when Maro couldn't hear. But there hadn't been the opportunity to discuss it properly. 'Actually, there was one just today,' I added, and then I figured I might as well go into the whole story about my conversation with the woman who was looking for Archie Booth.

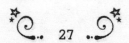

'So what're you gonna do about it?' asked Flossie.

I shrugged, drawing in the moist dirt with a stick. 'Ha! Well, I guess I'll keep an eye out for him. But actually *search* for him? Pfft. What am I gonna do, scour the whole of Ilkley Moor? As if! Anyway, what would be the point? No…just telling you, that's all.'

'Oh, Kitty, you've got to try harder than that!' said Kamal, his dark eyes all big and earnest. 'If you can help her, you must; it's the reason you were given the gift.'

Blimey. I was a bit taken aback by this, to be honest. 'Hang on; do you actually believe in ghosts, or not?'

Kamal averted his eyes. 'Well, I—'

'You think I'm making this whole thing up, don't you?'

'No! I…it's just… Look, I don't think you're lying. And anyway, what I believe don't come into it: what's important is what *you* believe. Don't make much odds whether it's spirits of dead people you're seeing, or jinn taking the form of dead people, or whatever. Point is, whichever way you look at it, you've been called on to help; it's your duty to honour that.'

'Hey, I'm not God, you know; I can't help everybody!'

'But you do help some ghosts with their problems, Kitty,' said Flossie, helpfully. 'I mean, what about when we were in—'

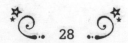

'Yes, thank you, Flossie,' I interrupted – but it was too late.

'Hold up,' said Kamal. 'D'you mean to say that some of these calls from the spirits are worth bothering with, and others are not? Why's that, then?'

Good grief! I'd known Kamal for all of about five minutes, and here he was, guilt-tripping me. Who did he think he was?

'I never said she wasn't *worth* helping,' I snapped. 'It's like I said before; it'd be like looking for a needle in a haystack.' I turned to Sam and Flossie. 'Guys, back me up here!'

'She has a point,' said Sam.

'Yeah,' added Flossie.

Kamal wasn't convinced. 'All I'm saying is, you should find out what you can about this Archie Booth. I mean, what if you saw him without realising who he was?'

'That's a fair point too,' said Sam.

'Uh-huh,' added Flossie.

Oh, for God's sake! 'Look, I *said* I'd keep an eye out for him...'

'But you won't actually investigate it,' said Kamal. He shrugged, and leaned back on his elbows. 'I dunno, seems a bit unfair, that's all.'

There was an awkward silence.

Then Flossie said, 'Hey, who wants to play Pooh Sticks?'

'What's Pooh Sticks?' asked Kamal.

'Oh, you each throw a stick into the stream from the bridge,' explained Flossie, 'and you race them; see whose gets to the other side first. Come on!'

Both Sam and Kamal got up to go. 'Kit?' said Sam.

'Ah, catch you later,' I said, chucking my stick down. I was feeling too rattled and confused just at that moment; I figured I'd just hang for a bit, think things over.

I headed in the other direction, down the narrow, crooked path through the trees. After a while the trees thinned out, letting the late afternoon sunshine in. Finding a sunny patch, I lay down and stretched out on the grassy bank. The strong wind of the last couple of days had dropped to a light breeze; it really was starting to feel like summer. Ah, the hell with it all. Here, I could have some peace. No ghosts bothering me, no brothers, sisters, annoying virtual strangers telling me what to do. What did they know? *They* didn't have phantorama!

I closed my eyes and soaked up the warm rays, while listening to the gentle rustle of leaves and the babbling

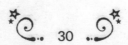

of the stream. Somewhere off in the distance, children were chanting. Bit late in the day, I thought; school would be finished by now. Some sort of choir practice, I guessed; the village was not far off. *Bah da de dada dada DUMM*, went the song, round and round, over and over… It was kind of soothing, actually.

The singing grew louder. A change of wind direction, maybe…except that…no, surely not? I sat up, looked around. Nope, no sign of anyone. Couldn't be coming from the caravan park: no kids there. 'OK, nice trick, now come out,' I said. But I already knew it couldn't be Sam and the others; this was a whole chorus of voices.

Hmm. Now it was starting to bug me. Where *was* it coming from?

Then, *whoosh*: the voices rushed towards me, louder than ever, and now the words were clear as well:

'Where has tha bin since ah saw thee?'

'Whoah!' I jumped up, turned around. Nobody was there. Yet the voices were right on top of me.

'Where has tha bin since ah saw thee?' they repeated.

Then they stopped.

I stood there gasping, heart banging in my chest, completely alone. The breeze rustled through the trees, the stream burbled.

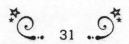

Then, '*Ark!*' I heard wings flapping and there, in front of me, was a raven – no, not *a* raven; *the* raven. The same one I'd seen the day before.

3

Missing Persons

I could tell it was the same bird. Don't ask me how: I just *knew*.

Staring at it, I took a step backwards. Now, it's not like I'm phobic or anything; I can't explain why it creeped me out so much, but it did. That shiny little black eye just seemed to pierce my soul; it felt as if the raven was inhabited by some powerful spirit, and it made me go cold all over.

I took another step backwards. 'What do you want?' I asked out loud.

'Kitty?' said a voice.

'Waah!' I cried, arms flailing as I turned, and saw Sam standing there.

'Whoah, sorry, didn't mean to make you jump,' said Sam. 'Er…were you talking to someone just now? Was there a ghost?'

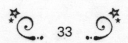

I shook my head, trying to reset my brain. 'Yeah… I mean, no. I mean… It's just that, yes, you made me jump.' I didn't want to let on about the raven – which was still in exactly the same spot – because then Sam would just have an excuse to gloat, making out that I was freaked out by that Hitchcock movie, which I wasn't. 'Where's Kamal?'

'Gone back to look after his sister,' said Flossie, now catching up.

'Sorry I made you jump,' said Sam. 'It's just…are you *sure* there was no ghost? I could swear I heard you talking.'

'No, you didn't.'

His gaze travelled over to the raven, then back to me. 'OK!' he said at last. 'I guess not.'

I stared hard at the ground until, to my relief, I heard the raven flap away.

FRIDAY 3 JUNE

I am not being paranoid: that raven is targeting me. What is going on? It's not a ghost bird – that's for sure, 'cause others have seen it. But it is spooky. The way it STARES at me! And now there's the VOICES. OK, they're not actually coming from the raven – but there's

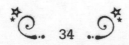

a connection, I know there is. Don't ask me how I know, I just do.

'Where has tha been since ah saw thee?'

Those were the words in the song I heard. I think it's Yorkshire for 'Where have you been since I saw you?' So, I guess I'm meant to take note of this somehow. OK, note taken. Next?

Is it linked to Archie Booth?

Maybe. Maybe not.

I Am SO. FED UP. WITH GHOSTS.

All they ever do is nag. It's bad enough that I've got people like Kamal guilt-tripping me. When exactly did my phantorama turn into a JOB, btw?! One that INCIDENTALLY I never applied for, don't get paid for, never even get a day off. I DESERVE a day off once in a while!

Actually, maybe I should start charging for my services. How about that? Only…SLIGHT problem: all my 'clients' are ghosts themselves. FAIL! 'OK, Mrs Booth, I'll try and track down your Archie; that'll be £200 plus expenses.' RIIIGHT. It's not fair. I mean, it's not like I don't want to know where these missing people have got to. I just wish someone ELSE would figure things out once in a while…

SO: here's what I know so far about Archie:

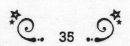

- Last seen on Ilkley Moor, probably some time in the 1960s.
- Chunky kid.
- Was wearing a 'donkey jacket'. According to Sam, it's the sort road workers wear: black, with a PVC patch across the shoulders.
- And Doc Marten boots.

That's it. No age, no hair colour…urgh.

Maro wasn't doing dinner. 'The couple with the funny little van called Zoe are having a barbecue this evening,' she explained. 'And everyone's invited. So come on; let's go!'

I thought about all the people we'd seen so far at the caravan park, and thought I'd rather stick needles in my eyes. 'Urgh. Do we have to?'

'It'll be bread and butter for dinner if you don't,' said Maro. 'I've made spinach pie, but I'm bringing it along – and no, I won't cut off a piece first.'

'Come on,' said Flossie. 'We might as well.'

'Oh, OK,' I groaned. Looking on the bright side, maybe the dead 60s guy would be there. Then I thought, wow: it says something about a party if the only person

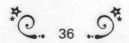

you're looking forward to seeing there is a dead one…

So off we went. Maro led the way Greek-lady style, laden with foil-covered food. You have to bring foil-covered food to a party if you're a Greek lady; it's the law.

The dead 60s guy was there, as it turned out. Vince, I decided to call him – just because he looked like a Vince. He strode towards me, arms outstretched and beaming like I was his best mate or something. Well, I certainly wasn't up for a ghost-hug, but nor did I want to ignore him, so I figured I'd fob him off with a high-five instead. I held up my hand, then suddenly remembered a warning from Maro, the first time I'd developed my phantorama:

'Never, ever *link hands with a ghost: if you do, you may be risking your life.'*

I quickly yanked my arm down again. Did high-fiving count as 'linking' hands? I wasn't sure – but I wasn't about to find out. Vince blinked at me as I shot past; I shrugged apologetically at him.

Zoe's current live occupants were Cathy and Ben. They were quite nice actually – for adults. Cathy was small and round and talked like a wide-mouthed Londoner, missing off lots of 't's. Ben was tall and gangly, with a bit of a wicked laugh. They both had longish hair

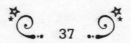

that was going grey and wiry; Ben wore his in a ponytail.

Brian was there too; other visitors were a little white-haired lady called Dorothy, and a bald man called Henry. The scary guy was there (the dog was asleep, I was glad to see). His name was Jim, and he was here with his wife, Kim, and their pregnant grown-up daughter, Kaylee. Mr and Mrs Zip-up Cardie weren't there. Neither was Kamal; he'd gone home, as his mum had already made dinner.

'I like that you called your van "Zoe",' Maro told Cathy. She pronounced it the Greek way: 'Zoi'. 'Any reason for that?'

'Oh, it's just a name we love,' said Cathy, as she laid out some bread rolls. 'And 'cause it's Greek for "life".'

Life – ha! I didn't like to mention Vince, Zoe's resident dead person. Life and Death: that's what they should really call it, I thought. Zoe and…hmm. What was the Greek for death? I couldn't remember…

'Oh, but you'd know that, of course, being Greek,' Cathy added.

'Mm-hmm,' murmured Maro, from behind her plastic cup of punch. 'Hey, why don't we paint *our* van's name on the front of it – what do you think, kids?'

'What's yours called, then?' asked Ben.

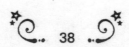

'Oh, ridiculous Greek name,' said Maro. '*Doureos hippos*; it means "Trojan Horse". It's kind of a family joke...'

'...But we just call it the Hippo for short,' added Sam.

Ben looked up from the sausages he was grilling on the barbecue and grinned. 'Do you sneak up in the night and ambush people, then?'

'Exactly!' said Maro. 'On all the poor unsuspecting family members we have scattered all over the place.'

'Only we haven't got any here,' said Flossie gloomily.

'Tell you what, *we'll* be your family for now, how's that?' said Cathy cheerfully. She pulled her big holey sweater round her. 'Ooh, it's getting chilly!' She put some more wood on the crackling fire; the sun was dipping below the trees now.

Then Henry, the bald guy, said, 'Does anyone know anything about this disappearance on the moor?' The others fell silent.

I felt my ears prick up too. How weird: surely he wasn't talking about Archie Booth?

'Disappearance?' said Cathy. 'Not heard anything about it.'

Brian smiled. 'Oh, it's just some chap, works at a bird

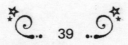

sanctuary near here. I'm sure he'll turn up before long…'

'No sign of him for a week now, apparently,' said Henry. 'Still no news, then?'

'No,' said Brian.

Only a week; OK, so not Archie. *Another* person who'd gone missing on the moor. I was just beginning to wonder how often this happened, when Dorothy gasped, 'Not another one!'

'What do you mean, another one?' asked Maro.

'There was a woman back in March,' said Dorothy, picking daintily at her piece of spinach pie. 'But they found the body soon after; they said she died of exposure.'

'That wa'n't exposure,' said Jim. Once he'd got everyone's attention, he puffed himself up, gesticulating with the chicken leg he was holding. 'Oh, that's the official line. What they don't tell you is, that woman was *mauled* to death.' Jim took a big bite out of the chicken leg.

Everyone gasped, including me.

'Oh, now, hang on–' Henry started.

'True as I'm sittin' here,' insisted Jim, with a sweep of his bull-like head. 'I've got a mate in the police, told me about it. Saw the pictures, said you wouldn't believe it–'

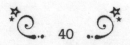

'I certainly wouldn't,' muttered Henry.

Jim didn't hear him. 'Would 'ave to be a terrible beast, to 'ave done that,' he added.

'Ah yes, the legend of the Barghest,' said Brian.

'The who?' asked Maro.

'The Barghest,' repeated Brian. 'It's a mythical beast – a big black spectral dog, supposed to herald death to anyone that sees it.'

'Brilliant: it's like *The Hound of the Baskervilles*,' joked Henry. 'What fun!'

Jim wasn't amused. 'You can believe what you like,' he said. 'I know the truth. There's been sightings of a *real live* dog out there; it's huge, and—'

Henry chortled into his plastic cup. 'Pull the other one!'

Jim made like he was going to lunge at Henry, but Brian jumped up and held him back.

Jim's wife Kim also reached out to restrain him, but she backed up his story. 'There have too been sightings,' she told Henry. 'We've read all about it. Haven't we, Kaylee?'

Kaylee nodded. 'Yeah.'

'Yeah, and there's been other disappearances, too – not even reported,' added Jim. 'Loners, like this latest one. Sheep have been killed, too.'

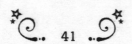

'Why wouldn't they be reported?' asked Maro.

'Because it's bad publicity, like, y'know?' said Jim, wiping barbecue sauce from his face with a paper napkin. 'Think about it: the moors are a big tourist attraction. People won't want to come, if they think there's a murderous beast out there. It's a big cover-up.'

'Where are you from, Jim?' asked Henry.

'Newcastle.'

'So why are *you* here, then, if it's so dangerous?'

'Because, *Henry*,' said Jim, shoving his big red face at him, 'it's only out on the *moor* you got to be careful.' He turned to his wife. 'We don't go out there, do we, love?'

'No…no,' said Kim, shaking her head vigorously.

Kaylee sat in silence, stroking her big round belly.

Brian stared at the ground, looking uneasy.

'Oh, I *see*,' said Henry. 'The wild, crazy beast waits for *you* to come to *it*!'

'Henry,' warned Ben, shaking his head.

'There is another possible explanation for the disappearances,' said Cathy.

Now all heads turned in her direction.

'Some of you will sneer at this, I know,' she went on, 'but the moor is actually a place full of ancient mystery. You only have to look at the carvings on the stones to realise that.'

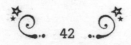

Maro had talked about these carvings, but we hadn't seen them yet; apparently they were gazillions of years old, going back to the Bronze Age or something.

'And there's one stone – the Swastika Stone,' said Cathy.

'Yes, it's famous!' said Brian, seizing gratefully on the change in subject matter. 'An ancient symbol for good luck.' Noticing the look of surprise on some of our faces, he added, 'And *not* anything to do with the Nazis.'

'*Sometimes* it means good luck,' said Cathy. 'And sometimes it's perpetual motion, or the sun...' She paused. 'But sometimes, it means a *portal into another world.*'

Jim snorted. 'Yeah, and pigs can fly, an' all!'

'What sort of other world?' asked Flossie, wide-eyed.

'Who knows?' said Cathy. 'There's some things the human brain isn't wired for. Like God, the infinite, the supernatural...'

Like ghosts, I thought.

'Well, I don't mind saying, I don't believe any of it,' said Henry. 'Not the murderous beast, nor the portal story – sorry, Cathy, but it is a bit far-fetched. And it doesn't explain the incident in March, because in that case, the body was found.'

'Well, that's true,' agreed Maro.

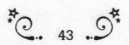

And so on and so on... Ben managed to avoid a punch-up by taking out his guitar: key move.

Sam, Floss and I left and headed over to Kamal's van. 'Whoa!' said Sam. 'That is some heavy stuff!'

'I really thought there was gonna be a fight there,' I said.

Flossie was all wide-eyed. 'D'you think that monster dog story is true?'

'Hmm, well, I know what Maro would say about that,' I said.

'That Jim's just blowing smoke out his bum?' said Sam.

'Uh-huh.'

'Yeah, but what do *you* think?' asked Flossie.

'I don't know what to make of any of it, to be honest,' I said. 'Tell you what: let's see what Kamal thinks. I knocked on his door.

Kamal appeared in the doorway. 'Hey.'

'Hey, you done with dinner yet?' I said.

'Yeah, why?'

'Good: got a question for you. OK, just suppose that every now and then for the past, say, fifty years, someone's gone missing on Ilkley Moor–'

'Oh, I saw on the news, there's some guy–'

'Yeah, we know. Well, what if there were others that

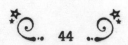

44

we don't know about – what if there's been some sort of cover-up? What d'you reckon it is the police would be hiding from the public? Some kind of wild beast? Or a portal that transports people into another world?'

Kamal laughed.

'I'm serious!'

'Ah, OK. Well, neither. Alien abduction, I'd say, it's gotta be.'

'You are *not* taking this seriously!'

'I'm amazed no one suggested that, actually,' said Sam. 'Can we come in?'

'OK.' Kamal held open the door.

We followed him inside and huddled around the little table; the place was stuffy and smelled yummy in a curryish sort of way. We filled him in on the evening's events – all the time trying not to disturb his mum and dad, who were parked in front of the telly, faces glowing.

'Oh, hey, shush,' said Kamal, as the local news report came on. 'Maybe there's more about this missing guy.' A blurry picture appeared on the screen. 'That's him... Dad? Turn up the volume, will you?'

As the volume went up, the reporter was saying:

'*Fears are growing for thirty-two-year-old Neil Hatch, of Baildon, West Yorkshire, who was reported missing three days*

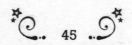

45

ago. Detectives say no one has seen Mr Hatch for at least seven days. We spoke to his employer at the Wharfedale Bird Sanctuary where he worked.'

A middle-aged woman appeared on the screen, saying:

'It's not like him to be absent from work with no explanation; he's the hardest worker I know. And nobody has been able to get in touch with him...'

The reporter went on to say that Mr Hatch had frequently been seen out on the moor, but that detectives dismissed any suggestion of a link between his disappearance and that of the woman whose body had been found there back in March.

'So,' said Kamal as the report ended, 'more homework for you, eh, Kitty?'

'OK, I admit it,' I said. 'I'm hooked.'

On the way back to the Hippo, we passed the Hippiemobile. The campfire was still going, and so was the music. Most people had left, but Maro and Dorothy were still there, and someone was singing – Brian, it turned out.

'Oh my God,' I said, stopping in my tracks. 'That song!'

'What about it?'

'I...I know it.'

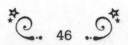

What I couldn't quite manage to say at that moment, was where I knew it from. It was the same tune I'd heard when I'd been sitting under the oak tree; the one sung by the ghostly children's voices.

On Ilkley Moor

It turned out to be a local folk song. Brian explained that he'd been singing it the traditional way, in the old dialect: 'On Ilkla Mooar baht 'at', which in proper English means 'On Ilkley Moor Without a Hat'. Weird song. About this hatless dude going to see some babe on the moor…then something about how he'd probably catch a cold and die, be buried and eaten by worms, and the worms would be eaten by ducks, and the ducks would be eaten by the humans. 'Then us'll all have etten thee,' it ends up, and finally: "that's where we get us own back" – though what they were getting their own back *for* is anybody's guess.

Weird. Bit sick, frankly.

Anyway, thanks to Brian's explanation, I now knew what those spooky kids' voices were singing. Well hey, whoop-de-doo: like I cared *what* they were singing! All right, maybe I did a bit…but what I really wanted to

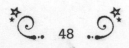

know was *whose* the voices were, and *why* they were singing it. Because there had to be a why: I was more sure than ever that this was some sort of message from the spirits, 'specially for me. Though I was still no nearer to figuring out what I was supposed to make of it.

Thinking about it made me think of that creepy raven again. What could possibly be the connection between it and the voices? At least it was only one raven…I hoped it wasn't planning on getting its mates to gang up on me. I thought about Neil Hatch, and his job at the bird sanctuary. Was it something to do with him? I hadn't a clue.

'Right, *pethia*, today's our day for a proper hike across the moor,' said Maro the next morning. 'So get on your hiking boots!'

'Ooh nooo!' said Flossie.

'Flossie's worried we might get eaten by the beast, or disappear through a portal into another world,' said Sam.

'That', said Maro, 'is the very reason we are going! I mean, we were going to go anyway, of course, as it's part of our local studies. But really: what a lot of old nonsense! There's no danger, and I'm going to prove it to you. Murderous beast, what a load of *femata*!'

'But…but…' Flossie's face tightened, her breath was shallow.

'But what, *Flosaki*?' said Maro.

'I'm scared of Jim!' Flossie burst out at last.

'Jim?' said Sam. 'What's he got to do with it?'

'He's…well…what if *he's* going out there and killing people?' said Flossie. 'Or getting his dog to do it?'

'Oh, *Flosaki-mou*, what makes you think that?' said Maro.

'Well, he's so…'

'Aggressive?'

'Yeah. And the dog, too.'

Maro patted Flossie on the shoulder. 'Flossie, I guarantee this is nothing to do with them.'

'Well, not that I think it is myself,' said Sam. 'But how can you be so sure?'

'Oh, call it grandma's intuition,' said Maro. '*O Jimmis*, he's blowing smoke out of *to bobo tou*, his bark is worse than his bite, trust me. And, anyway, if anyone wants to come after you on the moor, they'll have me to contend with, OK?' she added, with a wink. 'So let's go.'

Flossie stood firm. 'But what about Jim's *dog*? I bet you couldn't fight that off!'

'Floss,' said Sam, 'if Jim *were* killing people on the

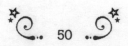

moor, he'd hardly be warning them to stay away from it, would he?'

'Yeah, he would,' said Flossie. 'Cause he'd want *less* people out there. So he's less likely to be spotted.'

'*Flosaki-mou*, I know his type,' said Maro. 'They love to spread crazy rumours, because they don't have enough going on in their lives. You honestly believe that all these mystery people who've supposedly gone missing just *happen* to be loners? Well, how convenient! And the woman who died back in March? The police wouldn't lie about the cause of death! It's nonsense.'

'They *might*,' insisted Flossie.

'No, Flossie,' said Maro. 'Whatever Jim says, it's in nobody's interest to let more people die – or sheep, for that matter. That woman died of exposure. You heard what Brian said; people can be stupid – and she was, it seems. I got the whole story after you left. There was a blizzard that day – not unheard of in March. And you know what? They found she had a broken leg. So they concluded she'd had a bad fall, wasn't able to move...and of course no one else was crazy enough to be out on the moor that day. She had no phone on her. You can see how it would have happened.'

'Well, what about this new guy, this Neil Hatch?' asked Flossie.

Maro sighed. 'People go missing all the time in London; you never worried about that when we lived there. Now, come on, *piyenoume*, let's go!'

Finally, Flossie agreed, and we got ready to leave.

'Right,' said Maro, looking faintly ridiculous in her hiking-boots-and-leggings combo. She was all kitted out with backpack, plastic map-holder thingy slung round her neck and wraparound shades. Anyone would think she was leading an expedition to the summit of Mount Snowdon, not just across Ilkley Moor. 'Let's go!' she announced, and off she swished in her all-weather hiking jacket.

We started out at the Cow and Calf, same as before. While Maro took the long, easy way round to the top, the rest of us scrambled up the more direct route; the craggy, rocky way I'd taken last time.

'You feeling better about this now, Floss?' I asked, as I helped her up a steep bit.

'Not really,' said Flossie, pausing to brush the dirt off her hands. 'I mean, there still could be other deaths we don't know about. And what about that boy Archie, who that ghosty lady was bugging you about? For all you know, *he* might have been murdered.'

'Floss, if Archie was killed it must've been, like, fifty years ago or something. Jim couldn't have had

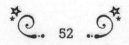

anything to do with that.'

'Kitty's right,' said Sam, 'and even if there was any truth in Jim's theory about a cover-up, why would they have reported what happened to that woman back in March?'

'Because they'd have to report things once in a while,' said Flossie, 'to make it look realistic.'

'You've got an answer for everything, Floss!' said Sam.

'Well, anyway,' I said, 'we still don't know whether this Neil Hatch is alive or not. I could try focusing on him, see if I can summon his ghost. If nothing happens, we still won't know if he's alive or dead…but if his ghost does appear, not only will we know for sure he's dead, but we might be able to find out how and why he died.'

'What about Archie, though?' asked Sam. 'Aren't you meant to be looking for him? Can you do both at once?'

'Well, no, I can't,' I said.

'Stop it, Sam,' said Flossie. 'I want Kitty to concentrate on Hatch; I wanna know what happened to him. I don't care about Archie.'

'Hang on a minute!' I said. 'I'm not some sort of supernatural Rent-a-Sleuth, you know! I'll do what *I* think's best.'

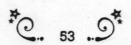

'Fine, ignore me then!' said Flossie. 'I just don't want anyone else to be murdered, that's all.'

'Argh! There isn't any–'

We were interrupted by a sharp cry, coming from the direction of the main path.

'It's Maro!' said Sam, pointing to where a small, white-haired figure was on the ground, attracting the attention of other walkers.

'Oh no!' cried Flossie. 'I knew it; she's been attacked!'

'No way. She must've fallen,' said Sam.

'Maro, we're coming!' I yelled, and the three of us scrambled over to where she was sitting.

'I'm sure she's OK, Floss,' said Sam as we went. 'She couldn't have been attacked, not with all these people around.'

By the time we arrived, a man was helping her to her feet. 'Oh, thank you, thank you,' said Maro, all flushed in the face, and swearing in Greek under her breath. 'I'll be all right now. Thank you,' she said, and the man went on his way.

Maro took a step, then winced in pain, and leaned on me and Sam. 'Oh, *pethakia*, I can't go on... I think I've strained it.'

'You mean *sprained*,' said Sam.

'Yes, strained,' said Maro, who still had some holes

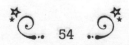

54

in her English, even after all these years.

'We'd better get you back down to the car park then,' said Sam.

Maro nodded. 'I'm sorry, *pethakia*.'

'It's OK, Maro,' said Flossie, obviously relieved.

Maro pulled the dangly map-holder off from around her neck and handed it to me. 'Well: won't be needing this any more. Ay-ay ay…ow!'

We'd almost got to the bottom of the path, when a voice said, 'Hello there!' We turned around and saw Brian from the caravan park, coming up behind us. 'Is everything all right?' he asked.

'Oh, yes, fine!' said Maro, with typically fake brightness.

Brian peered at her.

'Well,' she added, 'just a strained ankle, that's all.'

'She means "sprained",' said Sam. 'She fell over.'

'I twisted it!' added Maro. 'So silly!'

Brian looked concerned. 'You'd better get to A&E, have it X-rayed,' he said. 'D'you know where the hospital is?'

Maro shook her head vigorously. 'Oh, no need for such a fuss, nothing broken!'

'Now now, you can't be too careful,' said Brian. 'Tell you what: I could take you there–'

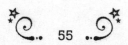

'Oh, really, I'll be fine,' protested Maro.

'It's no trouble,' insisted Brian. 'I was just heading home; it's on the way. Only...' He looked at the rest of us. 'Back of the car's full of stuff at the moment.'

'Oh that's OK,' I said quickly. 'We can get the bus back.' An idea was brewing in the back of my mind...

Brian glanced from us to Maro. 'Are you sure?'

'OK, maybe that's best,' said Maro at last. 'They know the way – don't you, *pethakia*? We did the journey just yesterday,' she told Brian. 'Look, you can even see the bus stop from here – easy! OK, kids, I'll see you back at the Hippo.'

We hugged, and they went on their way. 'Guys?' I said, as we watched them leave. 'We're not getting the bus. I've got a better idea.'

The Swastika Stone

'No way!' said Flossie. 'We don't *have* to do the walk now; I'm going home.'

'Flossie, if you leave, that means we have to go with you,' said Sam. 'And I'm with Kitty; I think we should do it.'

'Two against one,' I added.

'But–'

'No, no buts,' I said. 'Number one: there's no danger, obviously, because we were going to do it with Maro. Number two: we have a map. We won't get lost. Number three–'

'Look,' said Flossie, pulling a water bottle from Sam's pocket, 'we've got hardly any water. And Maro's gone off with all the food.'

'We'll survive! Anyway, there's a mystery to solve; you *like* mysteries.'

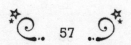

'Come on, Floss,' said Sam, more softly. 'You don't want to go back to the boring old campsite, do you?'

'But Maro–'

'Ah, Maro'll be gone ages,' I said. 'We'll be home by lunchtime; she won't even miss us. Anyway, now she's hurt her ankle, who knows how long it'll be before she's able to do something like this again?'

Flossie kicked a stone. 'Oh, all right.'

'All riiight!' said Sam. 'Let's do it.'

We clambered back up the rocks to the top.

Wow. Up here, you could see for miles all around; I hadn't fully appreciated it last time, what with being harassed by Mrs Booth and everything. To our right was the misty valley, with toy-town Ilkley in the distance. Everything else was moorland; a great green heathery sea, heaving with rock waves. It felt good to be out in the fresh air, clear my brain a bit; it had got all clogged up with thoughts about evil-eyed ravens, murderous dogs and missing persons.

Archie Booth. Neil Hatch.

Where to begin? I was intrigued, but now that I was out here, I hadn't a clue what to do. Wait for Stuff to Happen, I supposed. I thought grimly of Mrs Booth...

I was lagging behind. 'Which way, Kitty?' Sam called.

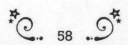

'Er…just keep following the stream,' I called back.

It wasn't long before we found our way to Landmark Number One: the ancient Twelve Apostles stone circle. A path of wooden planks led across a boggy patch to a clearing in the heather, where twelve hefty stones jutted up at the sky. Not huge ones like Stonehenge: this was a smaller, more intimate circle, with stones only hip height. But they were bold and solid, and leaned inward like they were having a conversation under the vast sky. Another little pile of stones sat in the middle.

'Yay!' said Flossie, checking the destination off on her list. 'I think Maro'll be proud of us; don't you, Kitty?'

I smiled. 'Glad we came now, are you?'

'Er…yeah, I s'pose.'

I took out my camera. I was about to take a picture of the view to the north, when Mrs Booth appeared. Wandering through the heather, turquoise coat-tails flapping in the wind, calling, 'Archie! Archie!'

I tried to hide from her, but even the stones were no cover; once a ghost senses your presence, there's no hiding from them. She zoomed over – that's the only way to describe it, she *zoomed* over – and got on my case, grabbing me with an icy hand. 'Have you seen my Archie? Have you?'

Oh, here we go, I thought, shaking my arm out of her

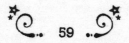

chilly grip. 'No, I haven't. And what's more, I'm not going to, because I'm on holiday, see? I'm off-duty. Sorry.'

Mrs Booth just stared at me with those deep, close-set eyes of hers and burst into tears. 'Oh, what am I to do? My boy...my Archie!'

She thrust herself this way and that, like a mime artist imitating 'grief'. Then, as she stood in the middle of the stone circle, wailing into the wind, the strangest thing happened: the twelve stones seemed to...change. The creases and angles of their surfaces twisted, rearranging themselves into faces. I wanted to move away, but it was like one of those dreams where you're paralysed; I couldn't move a muscle. Sam and Flossie also seemed frozen in time, locked into their positions outside the circle. Meanwhile, the clouds scudding overhead gathered and darkened; heavy shadows were thrown over the features of the stones. Their brows furrowed, their mouths gaped...and now there was a low moaning, like the whole moor was wallowing in grief. Like every spirit of the place from down the centuries since the circle's creation was gathered here at this moment, remembering all the pain they'd ever experienced. And the whole time, turquoise Mrs Booth was standing there in the middle, headscarf flapping.

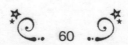

The moaning grew louder and louder. It went on for what seemed like an age, but was probably no more than about a minute. Then it just…stopped. The sky was bright again; Mrs Booth was gone, and the stones had flat, featureless faces. Sam and Floss carried on as before.

I just stood there, panting, gazing all around.

Suddenly, a little voice called, 'Hee-hee-hee-hee!' and a large bird came flapping noisily out of the heather.

'Aargh!' I cried, stepping back and falling over the pile of rocks that sat in the middle of the stone circle.

'Hey, Kitty, are you all right?' called Sam, running over.

'God, Sam, there's something creepy, something *evil*, in there!' I shrieked, pointing to the spot where the bird had come from.

'That?' said Sam. 'It was just a grouse, Kit.'

'No, no…in *there*.' Fear gripped me, tightening my chest. 'It's giggling! You probably can't hear it, it's probably–'

'I *did* hear it, Kitty,' said Sam. 'It was the grouse. That's its call. Didn't you go through the stuff Maro gave us to read up on? They're all over the moor, apparently.'

I hadn't read the stuff, not being a swot like Sam. 'Its call?'

'Yes, Kit.'

'Oh, its *call*!' I began to laugh. I laughed so much, I actually became quite hysterical.

'Hey, what's up?' asked Sam. 'Are you OK?'

'Yeah, I'm fine, it's just...' I glanced back at the stones, and a shiver ran through me. I just wanted to get as far away as possible. 'Come on, let's get going.'

Well, that was freaky enough. But it was nothing compared to what was waiting for me at the other side of the moor...

'What happened back there, Kitty?' asked Flossie.

'Back where?' I said, nonchalantly.

'At the Twelve Apostles. You were really freaked out by that grouse.'

'I was thinking the same thing,' said Sam. 'What else was there, Kit? Come on, I know you; you've gone all introverted all of a sudden. Did something happen?'

Introverted: such a Sam word.

I sighed. I'd have to tell them, or else they'd probably think I really did have some stupid bird-phobia thing. And by now we were far enough away from the Twelve Apostles that I felt I could actually talk about it without dissolving into jelly. 'Oh, it was just Mrs Booth,' I said, 'banging on about her Archie again.'

'Oh.'

'And…'

'Yes?' said Sam.

'Guys, how old can ghosts be, d'you reckon?'

Flossie frowned. 'How *old*?'

'Yeah,' I said. 'As in, going how far back in time? Is there a time limit on them? Like, three hundred years or something? 'Cause you know, I don't think I've ever seen a ghost from, say, the eighth century. Or 2000 BC, for that matter. That is, not a *proper* ghost…'

'What do you mean, not a proper one?' asked Flossie.

'You know: with arms and legs, and everything.' And I told them all about the weird visions and full-on 3D emo-fest I'd experienced at the stones.

'Wow,' said Sam. 'That sounds intense.'

'It *was*,' I said. 'Like one of those Greek choruses Maro likes to tell us about at every opportunity. So anyway, I'm thinking: maybe after a few centuries, the spirits just sort of…go all random. Kind of undefined, and merged. Like layers of rubbed-out pencil drawings.'

'I've never really thought about it,' said Flossie.

'Hey, so what was going on, then?' asked Sam. 'Were they all like, *really empathising* with Mrs Booth? Or just having a general moan?'

'I dunno,' I said. 'But either way, I feel well guilt-

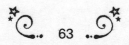

tripped.' I took off the map holder and handed it to Sam. 'Take over navigating now, will you? Next thing we have to find is something called...the Badger Stone. Here it is.' I showed him on the map. 'I'm going to see if I can summon Archie now.'

Well, I did try.

But it was hard; all I had to go on appearance-wise was the fact that he was probably a bit chunky, might be wearing a donkey jacket, and there was a fifty-fifty chance that his eyes were deep-set and too close together. But I still had no idea how old he was, how tall, what colour his hair was...basically, I still knew hardly anything about him. Hey, but I did what I could. And got precisely zilch. Nothing; not even the slightest glimmer.

As we carried on across this really desolate stretch of the moor, I switched to thinking about Neil Hatch. At least I had more info about him. I called and called to his spirit...I threw all my grey cells into it, and bunged in a hefty chunk of heart and lungs for good measure. It's something you have to put your *soul* into, like art or music – or cooking, if you're Maro. But up here, it was bleak and empty; no sign of civilisation in any direction – no sign of any ghosts, either. Just the occasional grouse, going 'Hee-hee-hee!' as it flapped out of a tussock of grass. And sheep. Black-faced, curly-horned sheep, staring at us as we went by.

'Why do they have to stare like that?' said Flossie. 'Gives me the creeps.'

Here, in this blustery nowhere place, we eventually came to the Badger Stone. To be honest, it was shaped more like a beached whale, or a sleeping sea-lion. Flossie ran her fingers over the ancient carvings etched into it: circles within circles, like targets, linked together. 'They're like great big googly eyes.'

'Yeah, that's what they are,' I said. 'Great big googly *sheep's* eyes, staring at you, Floss.'

She squealed. 'Noooo!'

'I'm thinking aliens, actually,' said Sam. 'Maybe Kamal's on to something.'

'Yeah, *right*,' I said.

'Yeah, you know; maybe viewed from the sky they're like, the alien equivalent of those big "H"s that mark where to land your helicopter.'

'Bit small for that,' said Flossie.

'How do you know the aliens themselves aren't really small?' said Sam. 'They could be no bigger than mice, for all you know.'

''K, well, right now it feels like we might as well *be* on another planet,' I said, rubbing my arms in the chilly breeze. 'Let's check this one off the list, and move on.'

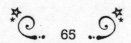

It was a relief to get back to a part of the moor where there were signs of life again. Now we were on a proper path, not trudging across a bog, and Ilkley town appeared over the horizon; other walkers began to appear. We carried on down the hill, then along a ridge overlooking the valley.

'Yay, nearly home!' said Flossie. 'How long have we been walking now?'

'Got to be over two hours,' said Sam.

'Oh, I am so gonna stuff myself when I get back,' said Flossie. 'I'm gonna have—'

'Hang on,' said Sam, pausing to consult the map. 'There's one more stone we still have to look at.'

Flossie groaned. 'Oh, *stones*. If I see one more *stone*, I'll scream, I swear.'

'Yeah, let's just skip it,' I said.

Sam peered at the map, then looked up. 'Oh, but we're here already.'

'We're where?'

'At the Swastika Stone; the one they were talking about last night. Maybe that's it, up ahead; see where the railings are?'

'OK, good, well, let's just go check it out, and then we're done,' I said.

We took some pictures of the stone and the swastika

carving on it – a sort of loopy cross-shape. Then we headed off, stomachs growling for lunch.

For some reason I glanced back – I don't know why. Maybe there was some supernatural force at work; not hard to imagine, given what happened next. Up at the craggy ridge where the Swastika Stone jutted out over the valley, I saw a figure standing by the railings. Not surprising: this was quite a popular spot for walkers. But this was no walker: I could see straight away that he was different. A boy, all alone, completely still, facing me…and he didn't look as if he belonged to our time.

Archie! I thought. 'Just a minute, guys!' I called to the others, then headed back.

Everything about him seemed to suggest it was Archie. Chunky-looking kid: check. Black jacket that might conceivably be a 'donkey jacket': check. He wore grey shorts, like old-fashioned school uniform, and his blond hair was cropped very short.

I sped up as I got nearer, excited. It *was* Archie, I was sure! OK, so the jacket didn't have the PVC patch, but apart from that…oh yes, it had to be him!

I stepped closer. 'Hi!'

He didn't say anything, just nodded slowly and held out his hand.

I honestly can't understand why I reached out my

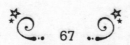

own hand. What the hell was I thinking? I knew I wasn't supposed to. I don't know; maybe it was the same invisible force that had made me look back. Maybe I forgot for a moment that I wasn't supposed to…maybe deep down I didn't really believe there was any great risk. Fill in the blank.

Whatever: I did it. I deliberately reached out to link hands with someone who was quite obviously a ghost. At which point–

Voom! I was yanked forward. Blobs and circles danced before my eyes; I hurtled through the air and slammed to the ground.

For a moment, I just lay there. Then, groaning, I propped myself up, my eyes still filled with psychedelic motes. I seemed to be down among the rocks that studded the hillside, just below the ridge where the Swastika Stone was; I could see the railings up above me. As soon as my vision began to clear, I got to my feet and looked around.

The first thing I noticed was this:

There was a girl lying at my feet.

And it wasn't just any girl.

It was me.

6

Lupa

I'd done something stupid; something Maro had warned me never to do, and like every stupid person in every fairy tale you heard as a kid, I'd gone right ahead and done it anyway; I'd reached out and linked hands with a ghost.

Dumb!

Really, really bone-headed and moronic.

And here I was, dead. Or was I? If so, what exactly had killed me?

All the stuff that happens in movies when spirits leave their bodies was happening now. Sam and Flossie peering down at me from the rocky crag above, waving their arms and crying out silently. Me hovering there watching, horrified, as I tried to speak to them, but they couldn't hear me. *The portal*, I thought, remembering what Cathy had said: maybe I had gone through the

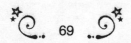

portal. Archie's ghost had just gone and yanked me through it, over to the other side – whatever that was.

Archie. He was still there, on the rock above. Standing over me, grinning.

'What the hell are you grinning at?' I shrieked. 'This isn't funny! I'm…it's…' I pointed at my body on the ground. 'That's *me*. That's my…oh, dear God, please tell me I'm not dead! I just need to get back *in*…oh please, *help* me!'

''Tis well and good,' said Archie. The way he spoke was completely unexpected, and his voice was small and high, yet kind of gravelly. 'There is time; you're not dead.'

Then he did something even more unexpected: he changed shape altogether. Became taller, slimmer…the jacket and shorts fizzled away and were replaced by a floral cotton dress with a Peter Pan collar and short sleeves. His nose and chin elongated, and his mouth widened. His hair grew darker and longer, and pulled into two bunches with big pink ribbons. He was now a girl – but a very, very ugly one. She had a shallow, sloping forehead and black eyebrows that met in the middle above her little shiny black eyes. Her wiry forearms and shins were covered in a down of dark hairs. She had a thick neck and pointy teeth. She looked like

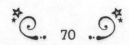

a Neanderthal child in a 1940s frock, ankle socks and Mary Janes. She even wore beads around her neck, which, frankly, only emphasised her ugliness.

I floated back up to her level – which surprised me a bit. I found that all I had to do was *think* float, and I floated. 'Who *are* you?' I asked.

'I have no name,' she said, still in that rough, breathy voice. 'I am as old as time. Well, nearly.'

Meanwhile, Sam was clambering down to where my body lay. It was only a metre or so down, and the rocks here were softened with moss; I hoped this meant I hadn't broken anything. Flossie was gazing down at my body, sobbing her heart out. Some other people had turned up as well, and a dog was barking and bouncing to and fro. All in perfect silence.

I turned back to Miss Neanderthal. 'And who was that before – the boy? Was that Archie?'

'Not Archie. I don't know who Archie is. I am Ernest for a while. One of my lives. You look for a twentieth-century boy, I show you Ernest.'

'Why? What…was that some kind of trick?'

Miss Neanderthal's face stretched into an expression of fake remorse, which clearly meant that yes, I had been tricked – only it was like she expected me to laugh and go, 'Oh ho-ho-ho, you tricked me into linking hands

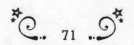

with you, just so you could yank my spirit out of my body…good joke!'

I was so furious, I might have exploded – if there was anything of me *to* explode. 'How dare you!' I said. 'Look, whoever you are, I did a dumb thing, OK? I let you trick me by pretending to be Archie, or Ernest or whatever, but…I made a mistake!' I could hear the panicky quiver in my voice as it went up an octave. 'I didn't mean to do it! I don't want to be here! So just tell me how to get back.'

'Worry not,' she said. 'You have seven minutes. Six and a half. Give or take.'

'Six and a half minutes till what?'

She didn't answer. Instead, she tilted her head to one side and gave me a wide, pointy-toothed grin. 'You're pretty!' She held out her right hand, palm facing me. It was a large, coarse hand with thick, curling fingernails. 'Friends?'

I was gobsmacked. '*Friends?* Are you kidding me?'

She whipped her hand back, folded her arms and turned away. 'I need not tell you how to get back!' she spat.

'OK, OK, you're my bezzy mate, whatever, now show me how to get back!'

She looked sideways at me. 'In time. You have the gift, Miss…what's your name?'

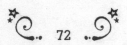

I forced myself to be calm and patient – not easy, with my brother and sister silently freaking out right beside me. 'I'm Kitty Slade,' I said. 'And maybe you'll tell me who the hell you are?'

'I am many,' she said. 'I live and die multi times, all over the world. One of these lives, the boy Ernest. But mostly I am Lupa.'

'OK, Lupa, so you managed to trick me into this…wherever we are…'

'The spirit world.'

'OK, the spirit world…' I'd kind of figured this out, but now that this one question was answered, it opened up a whole bunch of other ones about how this spirit-and-mortal-worlds thingy worked, exactly. But there wasn't time; I had too much else to find out in the six minutes or whatever I had left, so I just said, 'Why did you come for me?'

'You have the gift,' she said again. 'You need a spirit guide!'

'What? Why? No I don't! I don't know what you mean by that, anyway.'

'You search for a spirit, yet you venture out with no guide; how do you think you can find him?'

'I…I never thought of it like that,' I said. Was I just blindly bumbling about, like someone trying to cross the

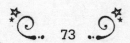

moor without a map? 'Well since I'm here, then…where is Archie?' I asked, looking around.

'Ermm…' Lupa looked around.

'Archie Booth,' I prompted.

'Aar-cheee Booooth…' said Lupa, scrunching up her tiny eyes. She reached out to me. 'Take my hand.'

I recoiled. 'No way!'

Lupa opened her eyes. 'You must connect with a spirit guide, if you want success. *Hand.*'

I rolled my eyes, and did as I was told. It was not as gross as I expected; in fact I barely felt anything at all. Then I realised that this was probably because I was currently only in spirit form myself; my body was elsewhere. We rose up and drifted, and I have to say, even though Lupa gave me the creeps, it felt amazing. Stuck in a lump of flesh and blood, you have no idea how *heavy* your everyday existence is. Right at that moment, I found myself thinking, *Wow, why the hell are we so attached to our bodies, anyway?*

Then we were down on the ground again, and Lupa's eyes were open. 'Archie Booth is not here,' she announced.

'Great. Like I needed you to tell me that,' I said. 'OK, get me back now, *please!*' Never mind the delicious weightlessness: I wasn't ready to give up on life just yet.

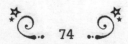

Lupa hung her head and pouted. She had very thin lips, so there wasn't much to pout with, but she did what she could. 'Oh, all right...' Then she perked up. 'But we are linked now: spirit sisters!' She took my hand in both of hers, pressing my right palm to hers, like you would if you were making a blood pact.

I wanted to pull my hand away, but I couldn't. 'Hey, do I get any say in this?'

'Spirit sisters!' repeated Lupa. 'We connected, and now I am freed!'

'What do you mean, "freed"?'

'I can now be with you in your world, all times. Not stuck on this side no more.'

'You weren't stuck here before: you appeared to me on the other side as the boy, remember? Ernest, or whatever. That's how you *dragged* me here.'

'Need the portal for that,' said Lupa. 'And for seven minutes only...no more!'

Seven minutes... 'Oh my God...what am I doing still here? Get me back!'

'Yes,' said Lupa. She reached out and motioned with her flattened hand as if she was feeling along a wall. 'It's somewhere around here...'

'Lupa!'

'Yes, yes, just a minute...'

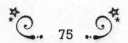

Sam was still kneeling beside my body, and Flossie was sobbing. Two strangers were with them now: one was trying to comfort Flossie, while the other was making a phone call.

'Oh! Here it is!' said Lupa. She seemed to be gripping something, which began to glow in her hand: a sort of blobby, amoeba-shaped thing. It grew and formed four arms...soon it was about the size of a car's steering wheel, and the exact same shape as the swastika on the stone. Lupa now used her other hand as well, and cranked it like it was a big handle; it turned slowly at first, then faster and faster, until it was just a spinning blur, its centre glowing brightest.

'Now!' said Lupa. 'You have to dive into it – aim straight for the centre. Go!'

Oh, wow. Did I trust her? Did I have any choice?

'Right,' I said, taking a deep phantom-breath. 'OK.' I braced myself, stretched my arms over my head and threw myself headlong at the glowing wheel.

Everything went black.

Saved Bacon

Light appeared, and shapes. Sky…faces.

'Ow!' I cried.

'Oh my God, she's back!' said a voice. Sam.

A dog started barking excitedly.

My whole body sizzled. 'Ow-ow-ow!'

'What is it, Kitty?'

'Pins and needles…all over!'

'Kitty, are you all right?' asked Flossie.

'I…I think so…'

A figure leaned over me, all dark against the bright sky – a woman. 'Don't move,' she said. 'I've called the emergency services; they're sending a helicopter.'

Helicopter: I knew that word, but what was it? For some reason I got an image of aliens landing a spaceship. Then I finally remembered what one was. 'No helicopter!' I cried. Ignoring the woman's advice, I stumbled to my feet. 'Ow-ow...I'm fine, really!'

As the blood returned to my limbs I steadied myself, leaning on Sam.

The woman peered at me. 'Did you hit your head?'

I shook my head. 'No...I think I just fainted.'

'Well, can you walk, then?'

'Yes, yes: look!' I marched on the spot, then reached up the side of the rock face. 'I can climb, too: see? I'm fine.'

'Well, we still need to get you to a hospital,' said the woman, 'but if you're able to walk as far as the road, there's no need for a helicopter.'

'Oh, I don't need to go to hospital at all, I promise,' I said.

The woman quickly made another call. 'Yes...yes, you can cancel it...I'm so sorry... Wait!'

It was me she was calling to, of course, because by now I'd scrambled up the rocks, back to the path. I didn't want doctors and nurses probing away at me, no way! I knew exactly what was 'wrong' with me, and there was nothing they could do about it.

'Wait! We'll take you to the hospital!' called the woman.

Her voice wafted on the breeze as I tore off, with Sam and Flossie following.

There were no broken bones; not for me, nor for Maro.

All the same, it took me the rest of the day to recover; out-of-body experiences really sap your energy, let me tell you. It was as much as I could do to walk the rest of the way home; then I just fell into bed, not wanting anything to eat.

'I think I'm coming down with something,' I lied. By now Maro knew we'd walked across the moor instead of taking the bus, but she didn't know about my little… adventure. Even Sam and Floss didn't know about my out-of-body experience. I couldn't tell *anyone* about that, not yet; I needed to get my head around it first. So I'd made out I didn't remember anything. As for Maro: turned out Sam had been trying to call her after my little 'accident', but she wasn't picking up. A few minutes later she'd called him back, having just got home and wondered where we were; she'd turned her phone off at the hospital and forgot to put it back on. Fortunately I'd come round by then, so I made sure Sam didn't say anything about it.

Sometimes, though, you can't fool Maro.

As soon as Sam and Flossie were out of the way –

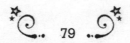

they went over to Kamal's – she brought me some hot tea, and sat on my bed. She was holding a small photo album, which she opened up.

'Did I ever show you this?' Maro asked. 'Most of my old photos are in storage; I hang onto just a few precious ones, like these. Your mama was…oh, not much older than you are now. Fifteen. We were in Italy…'

I was too tired for this. 'Maro, I–'

'It was a wonderful holiday,' Maro went on regardless, showing me picture after picture. 'Only one thing spoiled it: an accident.' She turned over the page, and there was a picture of my young mum, squinting in the sun, leaning against a rock.

I nearly spluttered my tea all over the album. Because there, on the rock, was a carving – almost identical to the one on the Swastika Stone.

I felt my face go all hot.

'This was taken just a few minutes before it happened,' said Maro. 'She fell. And although it wasn't a bad fall, she couldn't be roused. The really scary thing was, we couldn't even find a pulse.'

'Oh,' I said.

'After a few minutes she came round, and it was as if nothing had happened,' said Maro. 'She said she was fine, just…very tired.' I could feel her eyes boring into

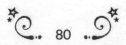

me. 'You would tell me if you ever had a similar experience, wouldn't you, *Kitaki-mou?*'

I thought about telling her; I really did. But somehow I couldn't. Like I say, I needed time to make sense of it all. 'Yes, I would,' I said. I bit my lip. 'So…did she tell you anything about it? I mean, did anything…?' I really didn't know how to frame the question, without giving away anything about my own experience.

'She said she'd felt compelled to link hands with a ghost,' said Maro. 'That is why I warn you never to do this…'

Yes, but I didn't have any choice! I felt like saying.

'After that, all she remembered was being out of her own body,' said Maro, 'and thinking she would never get back in.' She gave me another piercing look.

'Oh,' I said.

'Well, I hope it never happens to you,' said Maro. 'A terrifying experience…terrifying enough for her father and me, *O Theos kseri,* but for her? *Pos travmatiko!*' She kissed me on the forehead. 'OK, get some sleep now.'

Next day, I woke up at stupid o'clock, all bouncy and bright-eyed, raring to go. And *starving.* I must have lain there for about an hour, but my stomach was grumbling and eventually I had to get up and fix myself some

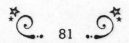

breakfast. I tried to do it silently, but it just wasn't possible.

'Urgh,' groaned Flossie. 'What are you *doing*?'

'Sshh!' I hissed. 'You'll wake the others.'

'We're already awake, thanks to you,' mumbled Sam.

'Sorry. Well, I'm making bacon and eggs. Anyone else want some?'

'What timezit?' muttered Sam.

I looked at the clock on the cooker. 'Er, five forty-six.'

'Urgh! Just…get it over with and leave us in peace.'

'All *right*!' I waited for my food to finish cooking – unfortunately, there's no way to make bacon sizzle quietly (or odourlessly: how the others resisted the smell was beyond me) – took my plate outside and sat on the doorstep.

The morning was white with mist, and deadly quiet; hardly anyone else was up yet, although one light did glimmer in what might have been Mr and Mrs Zip-up Cardie's place. I shovelled some toast and scrambled egg into my mouth, then paused as I heard a scuffling noise; a moment later, a dark figure appeared, looming in the mist.

A dog, panting hard, was hurtling towards me.

I'd just got to my feet and was fumbling with the

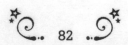

door handle with one hand, holding my plate in the other, when suddenly the dog jerked back with a whimper. 'Oi! Come 'ere!' said a gruff voice. It was Jim and his murderous mutt, Carlos – on a leash, thank God. After my bacon, no doubt. Well, not *my* bacon…at least I hoped not. And then they were gone. *Blimey*, I thought; they were up early. Unless…

No, I didn't dare think it. *Unless they'd been up all night, out on the moor.*

Revelation

SUNDAY 5 JUNE

Great. I now have a 'spirit guide'. Just in case I thought ghosts weren't bugging me enough. Lupa: weirdest looking thing I've ever seen. Hmm. I'm still trying to get to grips with this whole spiritual world/mortal world thing.

Before this happened, here's what I thought:

- There was the mortal world;
- and there was the spirit world.

And sometimes the spirits wandered into the mortal world, and lo, these were known as 'ghosts'. And their reason for hanging around was nearly always Unfinished Business; stuff they didn't get to sort out when they were alive. But mortals entering the spirit world? Never. Not possible!

That's it.

Only that's NOT it, is it? Ignoring the idea that Lupa might be a jinni (makes my head hurt), I'm now thinking there are other categories of spirit, besides the contented ones (i.e. the ones that stay well away from the mortal world) and the Tortured Souls with the Unfinished Business (i.e. the ghosts). 'Cause Lupa isn't in either of these categories, is she? She's not content...but it's not like she's got Unfinished Business either. I mean, she'd have mentioned it, wouldn't she? No: seems all she wants is to help me out, act as a sort of messenger between the two worlds...though what's in it for her, I haven't quite worked out yet.

THOUGHT:

What if there are CONTENTED spirits out there in the spirit world that know things that could help me – ones I wouldn't normally have access to, because they're not haunting the mortal world? But with Lupa's help, I COULD reach them, right?

OMG. I think I may be on to something here...

Finally we got to the library. Internet! At last!

Maro had asked Brian about the wi-fi problem at the campsite; he'd said he was working on it. To be honest,

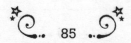

he didn't seem to care much about it. Anyway, everywhere we stay, Maro makes us go to the library for our 'local studies' sessions. Well, finding out about Archie Booth counted as local studies, as far as I was concerned – and it turned out, I made a couple of fairly major discoveries about him.

'He's not a kid!' I gasped. My voice echoed around the high ceilings; the librarian looked up and shushed me.

'Who isn't?' hissed Flossie, looking up from her moorland project.

'Archie Booth…check it out,' I whispered, pointing to the computer screen. 'This is definitely him: "disappeared in 1962, last seen on Ilkley Moor"…well, here's his birth date: 1941. So he was twenty-one at the time of his disappearance.'

'What made you think he was a boy, then?' asked Flossie.

'Well, I…I don't know, really. Just the way Mrs Booth talked about him, I guess. And here's a picture, look.'

'Oh, let's have a look,' said Sam, who'd also joined us by now.

The picture was black and white, of course – and fuzzy. Obviously blown up from a summer holiday

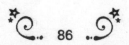

snapshot. Big, sweaty grin: chubby, kind of goofy-looking. Eyes too close together. Dark hair, short back and sides. Shirtsleeves rolled up, vest showing underneath. We read on:

The middle child of a family of five, Booth struggled at school and left at age fifteen to become a farm labourer. Booth was bullied at school, taunted for his learning difficulties; it has been suggested that he may have continued to suffer similar abuse in later life…

I felt a lump rise in my throat. 'Oh, poor Archie!'

'So maybe it was so bad that he killed himself,' suggested Flossie.

'What, and hid his own body?' said Sam. 'I don't think so!'

'Oh, right…'

'More likely, one of the bullies took things too far, ended up killing him,' said Sam. 'Maybe by accident.'

'Hmm…*maybe*,' I said. 'But in that case, what did they do with the body? It's been over fifty years! Hard to believe they wouldn't find anything in all that time. Look what it says here.' We read off the screen:

Extensive investigation into the disappearance failed to produce any result, and Booth was declared legally dead in 1969, seven years after his disappearance. His mother never gave up hope, however, and went on searching for

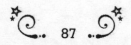

him until her death of a heart attack in 1975.

'That's the other thing I've realised,' I remarked.

'Sshh!' hissed the librarian. I gave her an apologetic look.

'What?' whispered Flossie.

'I'd thought this Mrs Booth was his grandmother, but she wasn't – she was his mum. She didn't die until thirteen years after Archie disappeared – thirty-four years after he was born. *That's* the Mrs Booth I've been seeing: the ghost of someone who died in 1975. She's only dressed like it's 1962 'cause she's an old person.'

'Sixty-nine when she died, it says here,' said Sam, scrolling down. He jotted some notes down on his pad.

'Right. Plus I'd thought she was looking for a young boy, so of course I thought, "grandmother".'

'*Poor* Mrs Booth,' said Flossie.

'OK, don't rub it in,' I said.

'Ha, well if Archie wasn't killed, I guess there's always the possibility he disappeared through that portal that Cathy was on about,' said Sam.

'No, he didn't,' I said firmly.

'Hey, you never know!' said Sam. 'Not saying I *believe* in it, but–'

'No, look…OK, I need to explain something–'

'Excuse me,' interrupted a stern voice, making me

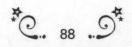

jump. I looked up; it was the librarian, a scary teacherish person with short, no-nonsense hair and piercing eyes. Her name tag said 'Barbara Hewlett'. 'If you're interested in that story,' she said, 'we've plenty more on it in the local newspaper archives. We've a copy of every edition going back to 1919. I can show you, but on one condition: that you *keep your voices down* – or talk outside.'

I felt myself transported back to school days; it made me queasy. 'Sorry! Er, but thank you; that sounds great.' I stood up. 'Um…we've got something to discuss outside; we'll be right back, OK?'

Flossie, Sam and I went out to the entrance lobby. 'All right, listen,' I said. 'I know all about that portal at the Swastika Stone; I went through it.'

Cue gasps of amazement, and funny looks from a passing mum with a toddler.

'I knew it!' said Flossie. 'Didn't I say, Sam? I *said* there was something weird going on there.'

'We both had a hunch at the time,' said Sam. 'Because of where you were when it happened…and because of your phantorama. But then we just believed you when you said you didn't remember anything. So…my God! What was it like?'

I filled them in on the whole thing; how I saw

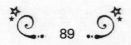

someone I thought was Archie Booth, who then turned into Lupa...everything. 'So obviously, things like this must have happened at the Swastika Stone before,' I said.

'But only to people with phantorama,' added Flossie.

'I guess. Well, come on, I can't be the only person in the world who has it; it's just incredibly rare. But even if this happens just once every five hundred years – hey, even if it's only ever happened once! – you can see how these portal stories would have come about. But the point is, it isn't possible for someone to *physically* disappear into it, d'you see? My *body* didn't disappear, did it?'

'I see what you're saying,' said Sam, scratching his head with his pencil. 'So that must mean that Archie Booth couldn't have disappeared through the portal.'

'Or Neil Hatch,' I said.

'Right,' said Sam. 'So even though the portal idea is way down here at the "highly unlikely" end of our list of explanations, we can now eliminate it completely.' He crossed it off on his notepad.

'Correct, Dr Watson,' I said. 'Oh, and don't go saying anything to Maro, OK? She'll only worry about the whole Lupa thing. To be honest, I'm a bit weirded out by her myself.'

'Sure thing,' said Sam. He chewed the end of his

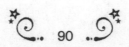

pencil, staring at his pad. 'Well, there is one other possible explanation – for Archie's disappearance, at least. Maybe he isn't dead, after all. Maybe he's alive and well in South America, with a different identity and everything!'

I laughed. 'Sam, don't be ridiculous! Poor Archie wasn't that clever. He hardly sounds like the sort of person who was capable of masterminding a cunning plan like that, now, does he?'

'I know,' said Sam. 'Just trying to think of every possibility.'

Every possibility. The words 'murderous dog' hovered in my mind; well, it was the other theory that had been put out there. I shuddered, remembering my early-morning encounter with the vicious Carlos.

Flossie noticed I'd gone all quiet. 'What is it, Kitty?' she asked.

'Oh, nothing.' I sure as hell wasn't going to discuss the murderous dog theory with my little sister. And it *was* far-fetched; bit like the Loch Ness Monster, or the Yeti. But then, up until yesterday, I'd have laughed at the portal idea too, wouldn't I? And yet, I now knew from personal experience that there was some truth in it. What if there really was some beast out there that no one had managed to catch yet? What if there really was a cover-up, and more people had disappeared than we knew about?

OK, Lupa, do your stuff, I thought, as I stepped outside the Hippo, just before going to bed. So she wanted to be my spirit guide: fine. Bring it on! She'd made contact with me, and I'd practically *died* in the process. So she'd better make it worth my while. I could certainly use the extra help. Back at the library we'd found the edition of the local paper that corresponded with the date Archie Booth's disappearance was reported in the Internet stories – and the following one, and the following one, until the story died out. But they hadn't told us anything new.

So I'd made the excuse of going for a short bike ride round the caravan site. I decided to head down to our secret spot by the stream, where I'd be less conspicuous. *Come on, Lupa!* I thought, as I walked my bike the last few metres and leaned it against a tree. *Where are you when I need you?*

She'd better come soon. Even now, with the days almost at their longest, it was a bit too dark for comfort – especially down here. I pulled my sweater close around me, kept moving. Funny how walking up and down aimlessly, you can kid yourself that you're not a potential

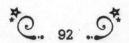

target for attackers. Like they're going to spot you, then think, *Oh no, she's moving about; I'd better leave her alone.* As if! Not that intruders could come this way; it was all within the secure grounds of the caravan park. So unless there was someone dangerous actually staying there, I was…

No. That was not a particularly reassuring thought. *Oh, come on, Lupa!*

A rustle in the leaves behind me made me turn around. 'Oh no; not you!' I said aloud.

Seven Minutes

That raven.

Curse that bird! There it was, all glossy and black, perched directly at eye-level, the branch still wavering where it had landed. Head tilted to the side, so that its right eye – always the right one! – was focused on me. The eye gleamed in non-existent moonlight...what *was* it that made it shine like that? The stream babbled away below...I could swear I heard giggles mixed in with the watery burblings: *hee-hee-hee!* like the call of the grouse on the moor. *Hee-hee-hee-HEEE!* And whisperings – *baht 'at* – did I really hear that?

Enough. I couldn't take this. I had to get away from that raven and its staring, staring eye, its black arrowhead beak, that sickening sense that if I met its gaze, it could make me drop down dead right on the spot. I pulled my eyes away from it – it was like tugging on dried gum – turned away, and immediately came face-to-face with Lupa's familiar pointy-toothed grin.

'Aah!' I jumped back. The raven flapped away.

'Hello friend!' said Lupa brightly. 'I wait for you, all day.'

I wait for you… I'd finally realised that Lupa never spoke in the past tense; everything was in the moment with her. Realising this made it easier to understand her: what she really meant was, 'I've been waiting for you.'

'You've been waiting for me? Why?' I asked.

She wrinkled her nose. 'You're in the city.'

You were *in the city…*

'Don't like city,' she went on. 'And your head all full up with thoughts, no room in there for me. Dance with me?' She held out both her sharp-taloned hands and cocked her head to one side. I realised she reminded me of a friend from when I was five years old. A very weird, very ugly version.

I shoved my hands under my armpits. 'No way! I'm not falling for that one again!'

'Only *dance*, I promise: like this!' I kept my hands hidden, but she reached out and took my upper arms in her coarse, icy grip; all of a sudden I was being bounced up and down like I was her favourite dolly or something, *boing boing boing*, while she skipped around in a circle.

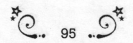

I felt unbelievably stupid, I can tell you. I tried to protest, but she wasn't listening, just singing breathlessly: 'LA-di-DA, di DA…'

Finally, after several moments of this – 'di-*DAAAA*!' – she tumbled to the ground, taking me along with her. She burst out laughing. 'Oh, such fun! We have fun times together, my friend!'

Intensely annoying though all this was, I knew I had to humour her, otherwise she might go into a sulk. 'Ha ha, yes,' I said, brushing myself down. I cleared my throat. 'Er, Lupa? About this spirit guide business.'

'I am your spirit guide, yes. Spirit sisters, my friend!' She held up her palm, inviting me to touch.

I didn't. 'Uh, yes…see, I want to try again, with Archie Booth.'

'No Archie Booth,' said Lupa, shaking her head vigorously. 'No, no Archie. I don't find him.'

'Yeah I know, but listen,' I said. 'I have another idea. You have access to the whole of the spirit realm – where the contented spirits are. I can't reach them by myself; here in the mortal realm, I only come across the troubled ones. But on the other *side*…maybe there's a contented spirit somewhere that we can contact, you and me, together. Someone that knew Archie, and could give us vital information about him, d'you see? Because no one

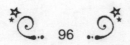

96

alive knows what happened to him.'

Lupa opened her tiny, crinkly eyes wide. 'Aah, yes, I see!' Then her brow furrowed again. 'No, not possible.'

'What do you mean, not possible?'

Lupa scrunched up one side of her face, an exaggerated portrait of someone thinking hard. She pushed out her lower lip, then attempted to touch the tip of her nose with it, going cross-eyed as she watched. Then she gave a little sigh and said, 'Dance again?' just as if I hadn't spoken.

I stood up. 'No!' I snapped. I was really mad now. 'Look, I don't *have* to spend time with you, you know. I'll…I'll spend all my time in the "city", and I'll have my head crammed with other stuff, and I won't…I won't dance with you again. You're meant to be helping me here!'

Lupa hung her head low and made her eyes go all pathetic, the way a dog does if you tell it off. I half expected her to whine like an injured hound. 'O-oh!' she said, to the tune of 'disappointed!' 'All *right then*. Need to work on it,' she added, studying her huge feet as she dragged her heels back and forth in the dirt. 'Very hard.'

'OK,' I said. 'How long do you need?'

Lupa counted her fingers. 'Five…six…seven. Seven minutes.' She nodded firmly on the 'seven'.

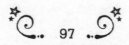

'Great!' I said, and went to sit down.

'No, no…not here. I come to you,' said Lupa. 'I know where you are.' Then she faded, and was gone.

Progress! Maybe. I hoped.

On my way back to the Hippo, I was passed by a grubby white car that I recognised as Jim's; ten o'clock, and he was just now going out? Not only that, but the car had apparently been rumbling down the hill without the engine on, because only here, where the ground was levelling out, did the ignition start. Why was that? I wondered. I made a mental note to discuss this with Sam.

The bike ride back couldn't have taken more than about three minutes; just another four to wait, I guessed.

'Ah, there you are, *Kitaki-mou*,' said Maro, looking up drowsily from her book. She closed the book and gave me a kiss. 'OK, I'm goina bed. I'm up to my eyeballs in medication, gonna sleep like a rock.'

Good, I thought. 'Night-night.'

Within moments, she was snoring.

Must be about seven minutes by now, I thought, peering outside.

'Whatcha doin'?' drawled Flossie sleepily.

I turned on the tap. 'Just…getting a glass of water,' I said. I did exactly that, then drank it down…still no sign of Lupa. Well, might as well make like I'm going to

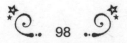

bed, I thought. I stripped down to my T-shirt and shorts, and got under the covers. *Any minute now*, I thought. *Meanwhile, I'll just lay my head on the pillow...*

Tap tap tap.

I stirred. What was that?

Tappity tap tap.

Now I was fully awake. The noise was coming from the window; I looked up to see Lupa's grotesque face leering down at me between the gap in the curtains. I nearly screamed, but stopped myself just in time, clamping my hand to my mouth. Of course: we had an arrangement. I checked the time: 4.40 a.m.! What on earth happened to seven minutes? I pulled on my sweater and my high-tops and crept outside.

'Hello, friend!' said Lupa, all jolly.

I frowned at her. '*Six hours*, Lupa,' I hissed. 'Bit longer than seven minutes, eh?'

Lupa counted her fingers breathily, extending them one by one. 'Four, five, *six*! Six is less than seven. I'm early!'

I groaned. 'No, it's less than seven *hours*, Lupa; it's a hell of a lot longer than seven minutes.'

Lupa, still grinning, nodded. 'Yeah: less than seven. Early!'

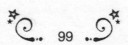

'No, you…oh, never mind. OK, what have you got for me?'

'I find a spirit connected to Archibooth, like you want,' said Lupa.

'Great! Where?' I looked around.

'No, not here; we go there.'

'Oh no – what, to the other side, the spirit world? No way!'

'No, we stay in the mortal realm,' said Lupa. 'But we must go back to the moor.'

'Oh now hang on–'

'It's very near!' insisted Lupa. 'At the waterfall, by the spring. White house there, not far from the Cow and Calf: I know it!' She nodded eagerly.

'Oh, man! Look, why do *I* have to go *there*? Can't they come to me?'

Lupa shook her head. 'No. She haunts only the sacred well. Not a portal, but spiritual home.'

'"Haunts"? You mean this is a *ghost*? I can connect with those by myself! So why didn't she respond to me, when I was out on the moor, trying to connect with Archie?'

Lupa shrugged. 'Maybe she don't care enough 'bout Archibooth to answer you.'

I gazed at her, seriously doubting whether I should

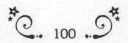

believe a single thing this bizarre creature ever said.

'Come!' she beckoned. 'Will take only seven minutes.'

'Right,' I said, sarcastically. I was beginning to understand that 'seven minutes' was Lupa-speak for just about any length of time between a minute and a day. 'Lupa, I can't do this,' I said. 'Not now, not in the middle of the night.'

'But it's morning!' said Lupa.

'OK, *technically*, but…' I trailed off. Actually, the sky was getting quite light already. What did I really have to lose by checking this out? I felt my pulse quicken, as I started to think about the real possibility of getting out there on my bike, and coming back before anyone else was up. No, that would be crazy…wouldn't it? How far was it, exactly? Three or four kilometres? With some hills involved. I could get there in, what, ten minutes?

'Come!' urged Lupa, grabbing my wrist. 'Let's go!'

'Hang on…I don't really know the way.'

'Never worry,' said Lupa. 'I do!'

Yeah, I thought; *if your navigating is anything like your timekeeping, I'm not going to rely on that.* But did I really want to go back inside and look for the map, when I might wake the others? No. Besides, I remembered Maro mentioning a café on the moor, when we'd gone

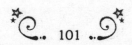

walking over by the Cow and Calf. 'The Visitor Centre', she'd called it; we'd nearly gone there but didn't in the end. How many houses on the moor could there be? I'd only seen one, near the Swastika Stone – but that one wasn't white, and there hadn't been a waterfall.

'OK,' I said. 'Just one more thing. This house; is it also a café?' If it was the same place, I thought, it would be signposted.

'A *what?*'

'Place-for-food-and-drink,' I explained. 'Refreshment for weary walkers.'

'Refreshment! Yes!' said Lupa. 'Come!'

'OK, but we have to use this,' I said, pulling my bike out. This would be interesting: my first bike ride with a ghost…or whatever she was. Did she weigh anything? I wondered. I got on. 'You…sit behind me; is that OK?'

'A two-wheel horseless cart!' said Lupa, clapping her hands. She rose up and parked herself silently on to the rack; I felt the chill of her on my back, but little else. 'Drive on!' she commanded, and we headed off.

The Drowned Girl

Never in my life had I been out at this time of the morning.

The chilly, damp air smelled grassy and fresh, with just the faintest whiff of cow poo. The grey sky dissolved into a bright apricot strip ahead of us, and a thick layer of mist hung over everything. The road was deserted.

'Whee!' went Lupa behind me. The cold of her hands around my middle chilled me to the bone; I wished I'd worn something warmer. I also wished she would shut up. 'Whee!' she went. 'Aaarrrr-ooom…hee-hee-hee! A-ROOO!'

'Lupa,' I said.

'Hee hee hee. Whizzy-whizzy-zoom!'

'Lupa, *stop it*, please. You're bugging me.'

'STOP!' cried Lupa; I clamped hard on the brakes, and we squealed to a halt.

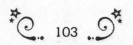

'What?' I asked, turning round.

Lupa looked at me blankly. 'You say stop. I say stop too.'

'Argh! I don't have time for this!' I yelled. 'Just...*be quiet* from now on, OK?'

Lupa nodded. 'Quiet: yes.'

We carried on, Lupa still yammering away, only quietly...it was hardly any less annoying. There was only one road into Ilkley from the caravan park; once we'd got to the centre of town, I knew the moor was to the right, so I headed that way. So far so good – and we'd only been out for a few minutes. 'OK, now what?' I asked, when we reached the moor.

'Straight,' said Lupa, and sure enough, a little further up the hill, we passed a sign that said 'Visitor Centre'. It occurred to me that I could have got there without Lupa's help, and had a bit of peace and quiet as well. And yet, annoying though she was...weirdly, I think I'd have been more scared by myself. Does that make sense? Probably not.

There was a deserted car park; beyond that was just a footpath that got really steep; I had to push the bike the rest of the way. It was even mistier out here – and chillier. The sweat on my back turned cold.

'Is it far?' I asked, huffing and puffing as we climbed.

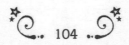

'Not far,' said Lupa. 'Maybe seven furlongs.'

'Riight,' I said.

Hee-hee-hee-hee! A grouse flapped up from the ground nearby; I jumped. 'I swear, I'll never get used to those blimmin' birds,' I said.

'Hee-hee-hee-hee!' went Lupa, imitating it. 'Hee-hee-hee-hee!'

'Yeah, all right, enough, Lupa; shut up.'

Before long I could hear the sound of running water: we had to be near now. The path led us across the small waterfall and the ferny gulley surrounding it; up ahead, a pale stone cottage appeared. 'Is that it?' I asked.

Lupa nodded. 'Yes.'

I leaned my bike against a tree, and we continued up the path to the weathered old mossy-roofed building. Above a doorway marked 'Café', a larger sign announced 'BATHS', and a black arrow pointed to a porch and another doorway marked 'ENTRANCE TO BATHHOUSE'.

'What's all this about baths?' I asked.

'It's the waters,' said Lupa. 'Refreshment; the spring. This way.' She beckoned me to the bathhouse entrance.

I held back. 'No way! Surely it's private property. Can't she come out?'

'Yes,' said Lupa. She nodded, then shook her head.

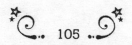

'No.' She put her face right up to the little wooden door, cupped her hand around her mouth, and whispered some words that didn't make any sense to me at all. Then she turned and said, 'I let you in.'

'No! I–'

I didn't get to finish my sentence, because before I knew what was going on, Lupa had melted into a puddle and slid herself under the door. I heard bolts clanking; the door creaked open, and someone or something grabbed me by the collar and yanked me inside.

The peeling walls of the stone-paved room went all the way up to the beamed roof; the weak grey dawn filtered in through the skylight. Set into the floor and taking up most of the space was a dark well shaped like a large keyhole, surrounded by iron railings. Other than some framed posters on the walls, there was just a large iron chandelier without any candles hanging from the cobwebby ceiling. A handwritten sign on the wall beside me warned:

ANY PERSON
ENTERING
THE BATH
DOES SO AT
THEIR OWN
RISK

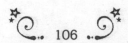

But there was no sign of Lupa – or anyone else, for that matter. Hearing a squeak, I jumped; a rat scuttled across the floor.

'Lupa?' I called softly. 'Where are you?'

Nothing.

There was a ripple in the water…and another. Then a pale figure slowly rose up out of it. It was a girl, with mottled blue-white skin. Her eyes were nothing but deep redness where the whites should be, and an inky blackness filling the iris; I'd never seen such dilated pupils, and they made her stare blank and eerie. She wore a white cap and a dress like something out of the eighteenth century. The water fell from her in silvery rivulets. When she'd risen so that the pool was waist-high, she drifted forward and up the steps to floor level; she passed right through the railings.

This was meant to be the ghost who'd help me find Archie Booth? Wrong era! Unless she was in fancy dress…but it didn't look that way. When you've seen as many ghosts as I have, you can tell; for one thing, her dress was kind of grubby, and ragged around the hem. Still, maybe she was an ancestor of Archie's or something; perhaps there was some kind of clue I hadn't thought about.

'Hello?' I said. Feeling completely ridiculous, I added,

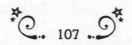

'Erm…Archie Booth? Do you, uh, know anything about him? At all?'

'Archie Booth, aye,' said the pale girl. Her voice was pale too: soft, whispery. 'T' shoe-mender, in t' village… Archie Booth.'

Oh, good grief. 'No, no,' I said, 'Not that Archie Booth! This one's from the twentieth century. He wasn't a shoe-mender, and…' I trailed off, as the black-and-red eyes stared back at me, clueless.

'Lupa?' I called, probably too loudly; I was really annoyed now. 'Lupa, where the hell are you? There's been a mistake!'

The pale girl came closer, her black-and-red eyes locked on to mine and I found I was transfixed. 'Come wi' me. Take to t' waters! They'll cleanse you of all ills.'

'No, I'll…' But I forgot what I wanted to say. Somehow the mention of the waters made me feel as if I'd suddenly found the answer to everything. *Of course!* I thought. *The waters: why didn't I think of that before?*

I was entranced by that black-and-red stare. And I guess at some point the gate to the pool opened up, and I was so glad, because those railings were in the way before, and now they weren't. And how deep the water was now! Before, a coin-scattered base barely more than a metre down…now nothing but deep, black, lovely water. Clear water – so sparklingly clear! – it would make everything else clear too…

Still the inky stare, pulling me along; then the figure turning, descending the steps, her skirts bubbling up around her. An annoying squeaking noise was coming from somewhere, threatening to break my concentration; and I *needed* to concentrate, because the answer was so *near* now, so *near*…

Down there in the well, the giant keyhole: *that* was where I'd find the key to the question, the answer to…whatever the question was, I couldn't remember just then.

But it didn't matter because I'd know it when I found it, wouldn't I? And I was closer now, following the girl as she descended, blond hair spreading out like sun rays, and down, down I went after her…

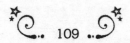

Murderous Dog

There was a hellish, bloodcurdling animal shout, like...
like the sound of a murderous dog.

Then–

'Kitty!'

I felt myself being hauled backwards.

Slam! I was on the cold stone flags, staring up at a
black-beamed roof, the cobwebbed chandelier, the
skylight. A horrible, ugly face loomed over me.

'Aargh!' I scrabbled into a sitting position, and now
the confusion left me, and I saw who it was. 'Lupa! Help!
The dog...'

'What dog?' said Lupa.

I looked around. There was no dog; there was only
me and Lupa. 'What...where did you get to?'

'I am here the whole time, but as a rat,' said Lupa.

'A *rat*? That was you squeaking? Why...?'

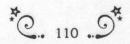

'I change; I'm a rat in another life,' she explained. 'I'm sorry. Get stuck.'

'Well, why did you change in the first place?'

'Anne – the girl. She's afeared of me like this.'

'Anne…'

Lupa threw her arms around me, and the chill sliced me through to the bone. 'Oh, she make hypnosis on you! You nearly drown!'

'Hypnosis? You're kidding me.'

'You don't remember, but look,' said Lupa, pointing to my legs, which were sopping wet. Ah, this accounted for the chilliness I was feeling at my other end, too.

'But I change back in time to save you,' said Lupa. 'I try to warn you in rat voice, but you don't listen.'

'*Save* me? It's your fault I'm here in the first place! Which, incidentally…' I realised I was raising my voice, so I lowered it to a whisper. '…Which, incidentally has been a *massive waste of time*, since this Anne whatever-her-name-is, is completely the wrong person, nothing to do with the Archie Booth I'm looking for–'

'I'm sorry,' said Lupa, hanging her head in that pathetic way of hers again.

'Well, why don't you check these things? It's… I can't…*ohhh!*' I stormed squelchingly out, slamming the door as I went. Whoops! *So* shouldn't have done that…

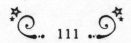

I saw a light come on in one of the upstairs windows. I really needed to control my temper; if I got caught out here, I didn't dare think what might happen. I hurried back to my bike and whizzed down the hill before anyone could see me.

I rode back, all pumped up with anger and irritation over the pointlessness of my trip; the risks I'd taken, for no good reason. Damn that Lupa! What had made me think she'd be any use? I was annoyed with myself, as much as anything else. Maybe now I'd be rid of her... although something told me she wasn't going to be that easy to shake off.

I was still annoyed by the time I got back to the caravan park, but by now I was energised from the exercise, with a pleasing tingle in my cheeks. Ten to six: still early, and no lights on yet in the Hippo – that was a relief, anyway. I'd half imagined there'd be a search party out looking for me; Maro might have got up to go to the loo or something, and noticed I was missing.

Someone else in the caravan park was up, though; I could hear footsteps. I hurried over to the Hippo door, just in time to avoid another encounter with Jim and Carlos, the dog breathing heavily and its lead chain clinking as they walked by.

I closed the door as quietly as I could, leaned against

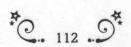

it and breathed in the warm, fuggy, sleep-filled air. What *was* Jim up to? I wondered, as I peeled off my soggy clothes. *Don't be daft*, I told myself; he was just walking the dog. What else would he be doing? And yet…where had he been going late last night?

Ridiculous though it was, I couldn't help thinking about Flossie's idea that he might be starving that scary dog of his, and setting him on unsuspecting walkers on the moor…only, even if you did believe that, he'd hardly be doing it at night-time, would he? No walkers.

OK, so scrub that.

Although…oh good grief. Now an even more disturbing idea hit me: what if he was going into town and killing people at night, and then dumping them on the moor? No. *Stop it*, I told myself. Something about this morning's bizarre events had made my imagination start working overtime; it was all the adrenaline, or something. But now that the thought was lodged in my mind, I realised something else: *how well it fitted*. Because he *would* want to put about the killer dog story, wouldn't he? That was exactly what he'd do. No doubt such stories were already around before; a ready-made 'explanation'.

I replayed the scene up at the bathhouse in my mind – the part just before Lupa reappeared. What *was* that

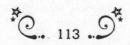

I'd heard? I could have sworn it sounded like a sort of growly bark, and yet there'd been *no dog*. How to explain that?

'So Jim likes to take his dog out for early-morning walks,' said Kamal, when we discussed things later, down by the stream. 'So what? He's just an early riser, is all.'

'Like, a *really* early riser,' I said. 'You do realise that both times I saw him it was around 6 a.m., and that was when he was coming *back* from his walk, not going out?'

Flossie shuddered. 'Whoo…he *so* gives me the creeps.'

I felt myself shudder; no, I couldn't say anything about my new theory. For one thing it really was a bit OTT, and for another, it would completely freak Flossie out. So instead, I just said, 'I know what you mean: I thought he enjoyed telling those gruesome tales of bloody deaths on the moor just a little bit too much.'

'Come on, Kit, plenty of people like gruesome stories,' said Sam. 'Doesn't make them killers! Anyway, how d'you know he was coming back: because of the direction he was going in?'

'Yes.'

'Not a reliable indicator,' said Sam.

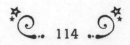

Argh, I thought. I knew he'd come over all self-important.

'Sam's right,' said Kamal. 'He could just be going a longer way round out of the park. Maybe he prefers it; maybe there's someone he wants to avoid…who knows? Anyway, it's not important.'

'OK,' I said, 'so he's going out at ten, coming back at six, and that doesn't seem weird to you? Remember, I saw him leave late last night.'

'You saw the *car* leave,' said Sam.

'Well, yeah.'

'Did you see who was driving it?' asked Kamal.

'Er, no…'

'Well, then,' said Kamal.

'You know, even if it *was* Jim,' said Sam, 'and even supposing it *was* the same trip – which is obviously what you're suggesting – well, he'd have come *back* in the car as well, wouldn't he?'

'Maybe he parked it somewhere else, so's to throw people off the scent,' I said.

'You know what?' said Kamal. 'I think you've decided something already about Jim, and you're trying to make the facts fit that.'

'I am not!'

'Actually, Kamal has a point,' said Sam. 'You're

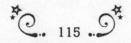

putting two and two together and making three thousand.'

'I…that's not fair! He—'

'…Is not a very appealing person, agreed,' said Sam. 'But you shouldn't let that get in the way. You want my advice? Concentrate on the facts.'

Kaylee

TUESDAY 7 JUNE

Concentrate on The Facts, Kitty. Yeah, well, I know everything there is to know about Archie Booth now, thanks to all those yellowing old newspapers at the library. Other than that, I seem to be going precisely nowhere with that one.

Back to Neil Hatch; he's still missing. Day 11.

Well, no more sign of a ghost there than with Archie, so he's either:

a) a contented spirit, gone to the place for Happy Dead Bunnies, so beyond my usual (i.e. minus Lupa) reach, or;

b) still alive.

OK, no way can he be a Happy Dead Bunny. Who

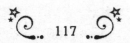

dies suddenly at thirty-two, and doesn't have Unfinished Business? Well, people who've killed themselves, I suppose. They'd be only too glad to be dead, wouldn't they? So say Neil Hatch did himself in: he wouldn't be a Happy Bunny, but nor would he be planning to kick around the mortal world a nanosecond longer than necessary.

Hmm.

What else? Need to get over my fear of that raven. It's trying to tell me something, I just know it. Even though it's not a ghost. How can that be? I should have asked Lupa about it. Ha! Like she's ANY USE at all.

Lupa. LUPA. Lupalupalupa loopy Lupa.

Lupa the weird girl. Lupa the rat. Lupa the pretend Archie. SHaPe ShIfTeR. That's what the jinn do, right? Change shape? So maybe Lupa's a jinni. Only, no. I don't believe in creatures made of smokeless fire. What I DO believe in is ghosts. She's just an ancient spirit, and...well, OK, I guess I now believe in reincarnation as well. As I understand it, that's how come she can be the boy, be the rat: because she had been them at some time in her existence...

HANG ON. The raven: what if IT'S the reincarnated spirit of someone that knew Archie – and it's trying to communicate that to me? Maybe it knows something

that could be of some help! I have to try and find out more…

As I came out of the shower, I was surprised to find Jim's daughter, the pregnant girl, sitting at the table with Maro. 'Oh! Hello,' I said.

'Kaylee just stopped by for my spinach pie recipe,' said Maro, who was scrawling something out on a pad.

'It's *really* good,' said Kaylee, stroking her huge belly. 'I've got such a craving for eggy cheesy things at the minute, and I'm reet bored of omelettes, you know?'

This was probably more than she'd said the entire evening, when we were over at the Hippiemobile.

Maro gazed admiringly at Kaylee's bump. 'When are you due?'

'July the fourth,' said Kaylee. 'Only he's that antsy in there, I'm not sure he wants to wait that long, do you, eh?' She pulled up her T-shirt as she spoke to her bump. 'Ooh…kickin' like there's no tomorrer; 'appen he'll be a premier league footballer!' she laughed.

I stared at her belly, not knowing what to say. My head was full of half-phrased questions I wanted to ask about her dad, about who goes out late at night, about

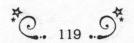

the stories of the murderous dog…none of it felt right, just now. Or, like, *ever.*

'You hope!' said Maro. 'Hey, but it might be a girl.'

'Yeah, it might,' said Kaylee. 'I don't mind which.'

'Well,' said Maro, tearing off a sheet of paper. 'I hope you can read my terrible handwriting.'

'Oh, cheers,' said Kaylee, looking it over. 'That's brilliant. Hey, I'll bring you a piece; you can give me marks out o' ten!'

'We'll make a Greek lady of you yet, *Kamari-mou,*' said Maro, struggling to get up with her dodgy ankle.

'Oh, don't get up, love,' said Kaylee, as she shifted her own great bulk off her seat. 'I'll see meself out. Ta-ra!'

'She seems nice,' I said, after she'd gone.

'Don't sound so *surprised,*' said Maro.

'Well, it's just her parents are so–'

'"Your children are not your children",' interrupted Maro. '"They are the sons and daughters of Life's longing for itself." Kahlil Gibran. There you go: poetry lesson for today.'

'"Your children are not your children"?' I repeated. 'But that's dumb! Of course they are.'

'"…They come *through* you but not *from* you, and though they are with you, yet they belong not to you…"'

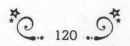

Maro quoted further. 'Think about it, *Kitaki-mou*. I won't tell you what it means; you read the whole thing, figure it out for yourself.'

Argh, Maro and her little 'lessons'. Why'd she have to load me up with *more* stuff to think about? Like I didn't have enough to try and figure out already.

Study time. At the library, we were meant to write some stuff from the point of view of a Roman, from back when Ilkley was just a fortress called Olicana. So there I was, trying to figure something out from books and the Internet, when all of a sudden:

'Kitteeee!'

I looked up. *Oh no*. Lupa! Now she was following me to the library? What the hell? I thought I was safe from her in the 'city'; was there *nowhere* I could escape from her now? Worse still, Mrs Booth was with her. My God: my least favourite spirits were ganging up on me. All I needed now was for that flipping raven to fly in through the window.

Lupa lumbered up to me, those stupid bunches of hers bobbing. 'Hello, friend!'

'What the hell are you doing here?' I hissed.

Sam and Floss shot me quizzical looks; needless to say, they couldn't see or hear my visitors.

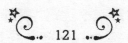

'Spirit sisters!' said Lupa, holding out the palm of her gnarly hand. 'We can be together all times!'

'Not here!' I growled. 'I'm working.'

Lupa perched on the table, slap-bang next to the computer monitor, while Mrs Booth settled herself in the chair beside me, handbag on her lap.

'Never worry,' said Lupa. 'We just watch.'

I stared at her. 'No. Go away, please.'

'Kitty, I'm sorry–'

'Not now! Another time...later.' I stared at the image on the computer screen: a female figure carved in stone, apparently some local Roman river goddess. I was trying to read about her, but Lupa was being really distracting.

'I try again,' she said. 'Other places I can look.'

'OK...whatever,' I said, hoping she'd just shut up and go away.

'I'm a good spirit guide, I am,' said Lupa. 'I help you.' She turned to Mrs Booth. 'I help you both. I find Archibooth.'

'Aye,' Mrs Booth, watching me as I made my notes. 'Oh look, she's left-handed, just like Archie.'

I did my best to ignore them, but they would not stop wittering on and on. Then Sam came over. 'Kit? What's up?'

I sighed. '*Guess.*'

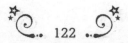

'No! *Here?*'

'Yup, Lupa *and* Mrs Booth. I've kind of ground to a halt here.'

'They used to tease him about that, an' all,' Mrs Booth was muttering. '*Cack-handed*, they called him…'

Oh, just *go away*.

'Sheesh,' said Sam. 'OK, well, let me know if I can help at all.' He peered at the screen. 'Oh, that's that river goddess. You gonna write about her, then?'

'Yeah…when I get my *brain* back,' I said, through gritted teeth. 'Can't hear myself think. Help me out: if this goddess had a festival, what d'you think it would've been called?'

'Er…dunno,' said Sam. 'The Romans had loads of festivals, though; should be a list somewhere. Seeya.'

As he went off, I did a search and found a Wikipedia page: Roman Festivals. Blimey, Sam wasn't kidding: those Romans never stopped partying in August. Must've been *so* much more fun back then. What did they do at Christmas time? I wondered. Something called Brumalia…Yeah, I was getting totally sidetracked, and who can blame me, what with the *non-stop soundtrack* of Lupa and Mrs Booth yammering on?

'The one…two…three of us; yes, *three*, we'll make a good team!' Lupa was saying.

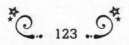 123

'I do hope so!' said Mrs Booth. 'He wouldn't do anything bad, you know, my Archie…'

Hmm…Valentine's Day… Something called Lupercalia. Nothing to do with romance; It came from the Latin for wolf, *lupus*.

Hang on. Lupus?

I looked up at Lupa. She was holding Mrs Booth's hand and rocking from side to side, singing, 'Arch-ee *Booth*, where are *yooo*…' She threw her head back and howled the last word, just like a…like a…

I felt the hairs on the back of my neck rise. No, don't be daft. All the same I found myself typing in a Wikipedia search: Lupa.

The page loaded oh-so-slowly. Then there it was.

Lupa, Latin for she-wolf.

'Ar-chee, Ar-chee,' went Lupa, swaying back and forth. 'Where are yoo-*hoo*!'

Aroooo!

I stared at that big head of hers, with those long, jutting features. The sharp teeth, the shallow, hairy brow… I remembered the dog-like sound I'd heard up at the baths, when it had been just me and her. Could that sound…could it have come from *Lupa herself*?

A creeping horror enveloped me. What the hell *was* she?

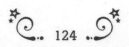

The Moral to the Tale

'OK, Lupa: no mucking about,' I said. We were standing on the pavement outside the library, in the pouring rain, and I could feel the blood rushing in my veins so hard it made me tremble. 'I wanna know exactly what you are.'

'I'm your spirit guide,' said Lupa, grinning her pointy-toothed grin. Mrs Booth stood next to her, nodding.

Murderous beast! The Barghest! said the voice in my head. But no, no, how could she possibly be?

'Why is your name Lupa?' I demanded.

Lupa shrugged. 'Pretty name! Why are you called Kitty?'

'Because she's like a cat?' suggested Mrs Booth.

'*Lupa* is Latin for she-wolf,' I said, grabbing Lupa by the arms. 'What *are* you, Lupa? Is there something you're hiding from me? Are you...' I paused. How

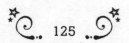

exactly should I put this? 'Look, you told me how you've been reincarnated many times…'

'Many times, yes.'

'Sometimes a human, sometimes a rat…'

'Yes, ancient spirit!' Lupa nodded.

'OK, well…' I'd hoped she might volunteer some information, but it didn't happen. Should I just say it outright? Hell, yes! I had my personal safety to think of! And then there was Neil Hatch, still missing… Finally, I blurted it out: 'Look, are you part wolf, or what?'

Lupa gazed at me, startled. She pulled away; her face crumpled, and she began to cry. 'I know I'm not pretty like you, but you're being cruel now!' She gave a great throaty sob, mouth wide open, snot spilling out of her nose and merging with the rain.

'You should be ashamed of yourself, name-calling like that!' said Mrs Booth.

'No, no, it's not name-calling, I'm–'

'Oh aye, I know your type,' interrupted Mrs Booth, eyes blazing with fury. She waggled a white-gloved finger at me. 'Used to come after my Archie, they did. Bullies! Taunting, singing those vicious songs…'

'No, I promise! It's–'

'AUWOOOO!' howled Lupa, more distressed than ever.

Mrs Booth wouldn't let me get a word in edgeways. 'We'll see how you like it, when you're on the receiving end!' she warned, then put a protective arm around Lupa. 'Don't you stand for it; seems we were wrong about this lass. Come on!' And together they fizzled away before my eyes.

'No, wait…come back!' I cried, but I was left just calling into the rain, like a lunatic. A passing woman with an umbrella gave me a weird look, and turned round to see who I was talking to.

'Kitty?' called Flossie from the library door. 'You OK? You're getting soaked!'

'Yeah, I'm OK,' I said. 'It's just…no, I'm fine.' And I trudged back inside.

OK, good, I thought. This was what I wanted, wasn't it? For Lupa and Mrs Booth to leave me alone. And now that was exactly what they were going to do. Result! Excellent.

Only it wasn't excellent.

Instead, I was left with a horrible, stinging feeling: a mix of rage at being misunderstood, and something that felt weirdly like sorrow for Lupa. Yup. *Incredibly annoying* though she was – not to mention possibly a murderous beast – I felt sorry for her, and wanted to

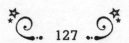

make her understand. No matter how much I tried to convince myself I was glad to be rid of her, that feeling wouldn't go away. Plus, I was now more curious about her than ever. No, more than curious: I was burning to know more.

The rain cleared up. Back at the caravan park, I took my bike out down to the stream, to have a think. The stream was gushing furiously after the rain, burbling loudly. At least Mrs Booth wouldn't be bothering me any more, I told myself; I was free to forget all about her Archie now. Trouble was, I found that pretty impossible too. The whole thing was dangling there in my head; I still really wanted to know what had happened to him. And to think I'd had his mum right there, with me! I could have asked her anything I wanted. Instead, I'd just sat there trying to ignore her, wishing she'd go away. What the hell was I thinking? Talk about missed opportunity. And now she'd decided I was a bully; I saw again those furious eyes, that wagging finger. *They used to come after my Archie, they did…taunting, singing…*

Singing.

As if on cue, the sound of those children's voices surfaced again, over the burbling of the stream:

*'Where has tha' bin since I saw thee?
On Ilkley Moor baht 'at…'*

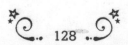

That song! Could I be hearing some sort of echo through time, of the voices of kids that taunted Archie? I wasn't exactly sure how that would work, but…oh, any moment now… I steeled myself for what I knew had to be coming next.

Plop. And there it was, on the ground beside me: the raven.

Its eye gleamed. A shiver ran through me. *'Tha's bound to catch thy death o' cold,'* sang the voices. *'Tha's bound to catch thy death o' cold…'*

OK: these things *had* to be linked, I decided. Whenever I heard the singing, the bird was there: this time, I just had to get over my ridiculous fear of the thing. What harm could it do me, for heaven's sake?

'You're just a bird!' I said aloud. I took a step closer to it. 'See? Not scared!'

'Ark!' said the raven.

'Aah!' I shrieked, and ran away and hid behind a tree.

'Then us'll have to bury thee,' went the taunting children.

'Bury *who*?' I cried, yelling randomly at the sky. 'Archie Booth?' I peeked out from behind the tree and forced myself to face the raven. 'Is this about Archie Booth?' I demanded. I might have felt stupid talking to a bird, but I didn't: that's how powerful a sense I had,

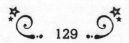

that there was a soul inside that creature that understood everything. 'What do you want?' I asked, getting bolder. 'What are you trying to tell me? *Is this about Archie Booth?*'

The raven didn't move, just went right on staring. The voices sang on, about worms eating the body, ducks eating the worms, people eating the ducks – but still no one appeared. Meanwhile I was locked in eye contact with the raven. Here was a spirit that couldn't talk to me, and yet I could feel it connecting with my mind... Yes, now I realised: those singing voices were *coming from the raven.*

Well, if it could send me its thoughts, then I could send mine back, I supposed. So I filled my head with the question: *What does this mean?*

The voices grew louder. *'There is a moral to this tale,'* they sang:

There is a moral to this tale
On Ilkley Moor baht 'at
On Ilkley Moor baht 'at...'

And then it came:

'Death to the dimwit Archie Booth.'

I clapped my hand to my mouth. The raven had answered me...and what a horrible answer it was. The voices were so loud now, I had to put my hands over

my ears, but the taunting rhythm still pounded in my head.

Then it ended suddenly. Silence.

I relaxed my arms and leaned against the tree trunk, turning away from the raven. They'd wished Archie *dead*? Why? My head was reeling. Had they killed him? But no…they couldn't have done. Archie had grown into adulthood. And these were definitely children's voices…it was a playground chant. A cruel, nasty playground chant, but nothing more than that. So what was the message for me?

'Ark!' cried the raven, and it flapped up to the branch beside me. I didn't jump this time; I was not afraid of it any more. Then it did something really strange. It lowered its head like it was going to peck something off the branch, only it didn't; it just kept its head hanging low, then began swaying it rhythmically from side to side. Something about the movement reminded me of a tiger I'd once seen in the zoo, pacing back and forth behind its grubby window. It wasn't idle pacing…maybe pacing wasn't even the right word: the tiger was *striding*, as if filled with a sense of purpose. Then hitting a dead end and looping back. Over and over again. Watching it had been unbearable, and had made my eyes fill with tears. How long had it been like that? Wasn't anyone

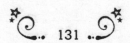 131

going to do anything about it? Anyone could see that the poor creature was going crazy in there, trapped inside its little enclosure.

This felt the same: a tortured soul, trapped this time in the body of a bird. Still it went on, jerking its lowered head to the left, to the right, to the left... This gesture was part of its message to me, I was sure. What was it that was tormenting this soul?

Then I got it. 'Oh! It's *you*, isn't it?' I said. 'You bullied him.'

The raven raised its head, then dipped it down low again, as if it were nodding. Then it went back to swaying.

Now I understood. 'And you're sorry!' I gasped, my voice choked with tears. 'You're so, so sorry!' It was all too much. I broke down and sobbed. For Archie, for the tiger...and yes, even for the raven.

On and on it swayed, back and forth, back and forth.

Arsenic!

THURSDAY 9 JUNE

OMG: can you believe it, the killer dog story's in the NEWSPAPER now! Well, the local paper. Big centre spread, grainy blown-up photo that you couldn't really make out too well, some sort of black blob with eyes. And above it were the words IS THIS THE KILLER DOG OF ILKLEY? Quotes from people saying there's a cover-up, like Jim was saying…saying it's killed two people and thirteen sheep this year. Other people saying it's a load of old rubbish. And the paper saying: 'What do YOU think? Have your say', etc… I tried to keep it from Flossie so's not to freak her out, but she found out anyway. Maro says if you believe that, you want your head examined.

OK, I'm just writing in here for the sake of it, because nothing has happened, ghost-wise. ZERO.

For five whole days.

I'm not counting stuff like sightings of my friend Vince, the dead 60s guy over at the Hippiemobile – he's just away in his own little world, with no insights on Archie Booth whatsoever. Believe me: I'VE TRIED. Been over there loads of times...Maro's there a lot, she's like bezzy mates with Cathy now. Typical Maro: it's nearly all old people here, but the one she pals up with is like, twenty years younger than her. Can't say I blame her, with the types you get here.

Neil Hatch has been missing seventeen days. They're still combing the moors. Most people not taking the killer-dog thing seriously.

NOTHING on Archie. No sign of Lupa, or Mrs Booth. Oh, and I told Sam and Floss all about the raven: the spooky singing I heard the other day, how it seemed to be connected to the raven, the gestures it made... They both think it's TOTALLY weird, but have no better idea than I do about what I can do with the information. I've seen it once or twice again, but that's it. No more clues.

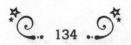

134

Why is it that life is always either really boring, or too exciting? It never seems to be in between: you know, just exciting *enough*. The day after I'd been complaining that nothing was happening, everything started to happen.

We were on a field trip to this local village. Kind of grim place stuck out in the middle of nowhere, all blackened York stone cottages and steep cobbled alleyways. Anyway, I'd just nipped into the shop – it was kind of *the* shop of the village, not much else there – and straight away I started getting a weird feeling. There was someone behind me; I could feel their eyes boring into me as I searched the cramped, dingy shelves for a packet of Hobnobs to take home. I tried to ignore them, like you do. And I couldn't find the biscuits, so I went down to the end of the shop where the chiller cabinet sat buzzing away, then back round the other side. There was an old man there, in a flat cap and a shabby beige coat. He looked up from the row of pickle jars and gazed hard at me. He pulled a little paper bag from his coat pocket, took a sweet from it and popped it into his mouth. His silver-stubbled jowls wobbled as he crunched hard on it.

I turned back, but by now the other person was there, facing me, in front of the chiller cabinet. She wore a headscarf like Mrs Booth's, but she was older and

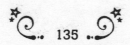

fatter, and carried a shopping basket in front of her like some sort of weapon.

I felt my face flush. I turned to study the shelves. Jam, marmalade, lemon curd...where *were* the biscuits? I turned a full 180 degrees to the shelves behind me.

The shop assistant finished serving someone else. 'Ey-up, love, we're closing now, can ah help yer?'

I looked up: it seemed to be me she was talking to. 'Oh, I, um…' It was impossible to look at her without also taking in the old man, who went on crunching and staring. And now three other people had appeared behind him, all giving me the evils.

'What was it you wanted?' prompted the shop assistant.

'Strychnine!' spat the man, glaring at me.

'Cyanide!' said the woman behind me. I glanced back at her in horror.

And now here was Mrs Booth beside her. 'Arsenic!' she shrieked.

Oh, I get it, I thought: *this is all your doing.* Seemed Mrs Booth had been busy these last few days, gathering her mates together so they could gang up on me.

I could hear her voice in my head: *We'll see how you like it, when you're on the receiving end.* Nice one, Mrs

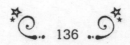

Booth. Though this wasn't bullying so much as full-on persecution.

Now the shop was full of them, all yelling 'Hemlock!' 'Sheep dip!' 'Paraquat!' and all manner of poisonous substances, till their voices merged into one great massive clamour – though it was clear that the shop assistant was blissfully unaware of it all. 'I...it's OK,' I told her. 'I, um...'

'Weed killer!' 'Rat poison!'

'...I forgot my money!' I squeaked. I tried to edge my way round the gang of phantoms, but there was no room to squeeze past. There must have been two dozen or more, all squished into that tiny space that smelt vaguely of cat food. *OK, they're only ghosts*, I told myself. *Not flesh and blood.* All the same, I didn't fancy trying to barrel right through them. The last time I'd come into forceful contact with a ghost, it had stung like a jellyfish. This would be like that twenty times over. Desperate, I peered at the half-open door at the end of the counter; chances were, this would lead out to the backyard. It was my only choice; I lunged for it.

'Hey!' called the shop assistant.

I stumbled through a gloomy passageway, stubbing my toe on a massive stack of drinks cans, and nearly tripping over some loose cables. I could feel the

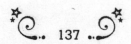

ghosts all coming after me as I barrelled through the tiny space to the back door. Grabbing the nearest object I might conceivably use as a weapon – a mop – I dashed out into the poky little patio. Dodging green plastic furniture, dead plants and fluttering laundry, I jabbed the mop back at the phantom crowd as they came after me, still yelling, 'Arsenic!' 'Sheep dip!' 'Paraquat!'

Out past the bins, through the garden gate, into a cobbled alleyway running along the back of the terrace. Finally, holding the mop up like it was a spear, I turned and yelled, 'OK! You've made your point! I *said* I was sorry, even though I didn't–'

Then I stopped mid-sentence because there in the crowd was a figure I recognised: a blond boy in a black jacket and old-fashioned school shorts. It was the same one I'd seen up at the Swastika Stone…the one that had turned into Lupa.

'Hey!' I said, moving closer. 'I know you!'

The boy shifted sideways, so that he was half-hidden by the large lady next to him. The figures surrounding him braced themselves against me as I went forward, grimy grey mop at the ready. 'What was the name?' I said. 'Ernest, right? One of your incarnations, *Lupa*. All right: you and I need to talk.' I came to a halt in front of

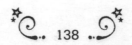

the crowd. 'This whole thing is ridiculous, and you know it. Come on, out!'

'You leave him alone!' said Mrs Booth, and the whole gang joined in warning me off, eyes ablaze with fury.

OK, there was nothing else for it: I would have to fight them off. With a battle cry that frankly took even me a bit by surprise, I lunged forward. 'Urgh! Yeargh!' I yelled, as I swiped my soggy weapon this way and that, but let me tell you, fighting off ghosts is not a very satisfying experience because they have a tendency to disappear before your very eyes, then whack you from behind. Which stings like hell.

'Some "spirit guide" you turned out to be!' I yelled at 'Ernest', still swiping and being swiped at. 'Don't tell me there's – ow! – *no one* on the other side that knows anything about Archie Booth; someone must do! You – ow! – you tricked me…I helped you into the mortal world like you wanted, and this is – ow! – this is all the thanks I get!'

I reached for him, but was left clutching at nothing as he shrank from my grasp.

'Kitty! What are you doing?' called a voice from behind me; I turned and saw Sam and Flossie at the end of the alleyway.

'Nothing, I was just– *Ow!*' I leaned on the mop, smarting all over from the ghost punches. And the boy was gone. 'Oh, what the hell,' I said at last, chucking the mop down. 'I'm out of here.'

Heading towards my brother and sister, I could feel the others following. I turned and roared at them like a wild thing, arms outstretched. 'Enough already!' I yelled. 'Give a girl a break, OK?' And I stomped off.

Two women were leaning on the garden fence nearby. 'One o' them southerners, I expect,' said one.

'Aye, 'appen she is,' said the other, nodding disapprovingly. 'Not the full shilling, by t' looks of it.'

Mr Sugden

'Hey, Kitty,' said Kamal, as I passed his caravan on the way to the laundry room. 'I was just going to come and show you this,' he said, thrusting me a copy of the local paper. 'Came this morning.'

'Oh…thanks.' I put down the laundry bag and took the paper. The headline read:

HATCH FEARED FOR HIS LIFE

The journalist had interviewed a bunch of Neil Hatch's neighbours and colleagues – Hatch didn't exactly have friends, apparently – and it seemed they had been concerned because he'd been behaving oddly – as if he was afraid someone was after him.

'Hmm…not a whole lot of info here. "…Been behaving in an increasingly furtive and anxious manner",'

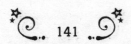

I read out, "'...recently taken to spending his evenings in the local pub, even though he didn't socialise with anyone...asking a neighbour to escort him home." I wonder who'd have been after someone like him?'

'Anybody's guess,' said Kamal. 'Says the police are continuing to investigate his private life.'

'Hmm...trying to find out if he had one at all, it seems. More stuff about all the hours he put in at the bird sanctuary...' I handed the paper back. 'Well, this is very interesting but hey, I'm not a detective.'

'No luck with the ghost search?' asked Kamal.

'Nope: nothing,' I said, picking up the laundry bag.

'Hey, you want a hand with that?' said Kamal.

'Nah, I'm good thanks,' I said, hoicking the bag on to my shoulder and wincing slightly at the soreness from yesterday's ghost scrum. 'Well, I've had no contact with Neil Hatch's ghost, if that's what you mean. So either he's still alive, or...or, I don't know. I guess maybe my phantorama isn't completely reliable. Or maybe there *aren't* any ghosts,' I added. 'Only jinn.'

'Do you seriously believe that?' said Kamal, walking alongside me.

'No. But hey, what do I know? I can't get Archie Booth either.'

'Maybe *he's* still alive,' said Kamal.

I sighed. 'We did this already. I just don't see how that's possible if…oh, wow,' I said, as Lupa came bounding towards me, crying, 'Kittee! Kittee!'

'What is it?' said Kamal.

'Well, guess what? My favourite "jinni" has just come to visit,' I said. 'Catch you later.'

'Oh, cool,' said Kamal. 'Well, hope it's something interesting.'

'It better be,' I said, through gritted teeth. I left him and continued on my way to the laundry room; Lupa lolloped alongside me.

'What do you want?' I asked frostily.

'I'm sorry for what is happening,' said Lupa. 'It's because you hurt my feelings.'

'Let me see now,' I said sarcastically. 'You misinterpreted a perfectly reasonable question I asked, didn't wait for an explanation, then let that old bag Mrs Booth get all her mates to gang up on me. Yeah, that seems fair! Oh, oh, and what's more, you *joined in.* Well, thanks for that. With "spirit sisters" like you, who needs…whatever the opposite of a spirit sister is.'

'I'm sorry,' Lupa repeated. 'But you say I don't help enough and so I try harder. And I find someone!'

'*Really*,' I said flatly. 'Like that sooo helpful spirit you

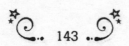

connected me with up there at the bathhouse. Well, thanks, but no thanks.'

Lupa jumped up and down. 'No, no! This one has an interesting story about Archie Booth… *your* Archie Booth.'

'Well, I'm very happy for you,' I said, letting myself into the laundry room. 'Why don't you just tell your *friend* Mrs Booth about it, OK? And leave me out of it.' I slammed the door behind me.

I began loading the laundry into the machine, but as soon as I put the clothes in, they came flying back out again. I peered inside: yup, there was Lupa, all curled up in the drum like a baby in a big steel womb. I chucked a towel at her, and it came right back at me.

'Listen to me!' she snapped, pulling herself out, massive feet first. 'I find a newspaperman!'

I sighed, sat back on my heels, crossed my arms and gazed at her silently.

'He's Mr Sugden and he's SICK and TIRED of hearing Archibooth, Archibooth all the time,' said Lupa. 'And he says lots and lots of bad words, like–'

'Yeah, whatever, Lupa,' I said. 'What did he tell you?'

'Right,' said Lupa, clasping her hands and gazing at the ceiling as she prepared to recite from memory. '"If I wanted to hang around wi' (bad word) mortals, I'd (bad word) haunt their world–'

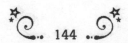

'*About Archie*, Lupa,' I said.

'Oh, yes. Right. Um, he says if I must know, he thinks maybe Archie still alive in nineteen…nineteen…'

'Oh, for crying out loud!'

'…seventy-seven!' said Lupa. 'Nineteen seventy-seven. Easter time.'

Right: you and your sevens, I thought, but didn't say it. 'Um, Lupa…is there any way I could talk to the spirit of this Mr Sugden myself?'

'Of course!' said Lupa. 'We can go now, if you like!'

'Go where?'

'To the other side,' said Lupa. 'I take you through the portal.'

'Whoah, woah…no, hang on. I'm not doing that!' I said. 'Can't you get *him* to come through it?'

'Oh no. Not possible. Only spirits wanting to enter the mortal world can cross over, and only if escorted by a mortal spirit.'

'So…even if he could be convinced, I would have to cross over to go and get him, is that what you're saying?'

'Yes,' said Lupa.

'OK, forget it; no way am I going through that again.' I stood up and began again with the laundry loading. 'Well thanks, Lupa. I'll, uh…yeah, thanks.'

She leaned against the washing machine and peered

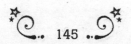

at me. 'Spirit sister? Will you show me how to be pretty like you?'

I looked into her doleful eyes and felt a pang of sympathy; she really was such a dog, poor thing. *She-wolf*... I shook the thought out of my head. 'Yeah, maybe, Lupa,' I said wearily. 'Just...not now, OK?'

'Very well,' said Lupa. 'I go now.' She hung her head, and turned to leave.

'Lupa?' I said.

She looked up.

'Look, thanks for trying, anyway.'

She shrugged despondently, and walked away.

I began again piling the laundry into the machine. *1977?* I thought. *Archie was still alive in 1977?* No wonder no body was found, then! And...what did that webpage say, when I'd looked him up in the library? He'd been declared legally dead seven years after he'd gone missing, in 1968 – a whole nine years before! They'd long since given up looking for him by 1977. So how did this Sugden know he was still alive at that time? And why didn't he tell anybody?

Oh, this was going to drive me crazy! I slammed the washing machine door shut, turned it on and ran out. 'Lupa!' I yelled. I couldn't see her anywhere. 'Lupa, come back!'

Immediately, she was practically glued to my side. 'You make me pretty now?' she asked eagerly.

'No, no…not right now, Lupa; it's the newspaperman …the portal. OK, I'll do it.'

'Good,' said Lupa. 'Come!'

I paused. I felt the panic rise in my throat. 'But I need, I need…' My breath shortened as I remembered the awfulness, the terrifying sensation of going over to the other side.

'What?' said Lupa.

Sam, I thought. I needed Sam. Just in case. But he was busy helping Brian with some weeding – and Brian was paying him. Flossie was with Maro, and in any case, she'd only freak out. But I needed a live person with me. This was risky! What if… *No! Don't think about that!* I told myself. Just then, I spotted Kamal wheeling idly along on his bike, looking bored. 'Kamal!' I called.

It was really uncomfortable on the back of Kamal's bike. My bum went numb, perched on that steel rack. My brain nearly went numb too, as I deliberately filled it with the stupidest song lyrics I could think of, just so I wouldn't think too much about what I was about to do, and lose my nerve.

Kamal was just really excited. 'So this jinni, it's right here with us now?'

I'd given up telling him Lupa wasn't a jinni. 'Sort of. But I told her the only way I was doing this was if she stayed silent and invisible: she drove me nuts last time.'

'Last time?'

'Yeah...never mind. But she's sticking by, in case I need her help getting there. I know the way, though; I just wish there was a short cut, but there isn't.'

"S OK,' said Kamal. 'I'm fast.'

'Just as well,' I said, shifting my bum. As we went, I explained to him what to expect when I went through the portal. 'Don't freak out, OK?' I said. 'I'll make sure I do it when no one's around, but after that there's bound to be people about, so...best thing is if you just lie next to me, like we're just, you know, chilling. Basking in the...sun.' I gazed hopefully at the sky.

As we got nearer to the Swastika Stone, I started to feel queasy. By the time I was actually standing in front of it, faced with that swirly pattern etched into the rock, I'd lost my nerve. 'No!' I cried. 'I must be out of my mind! I–'

But before I knew what was happening, Lupa had appeared in front of me, grabbed my hand and *voom!* Blackness and stars.

The Sheepshearer

'This 'er, then?' said a voice.

Gradually everything came into focus, and I saw a sallow-skinned, grumpy-looking old man, in a grubby snot-green coat, sitting on a rock, smoking a pipe. His name was Sugden.

'My spirit sister, yes!' said Lupa. 'She has just seven minutes.'

'Wanting to know about Archie Booth, eh?'

'Y-yes,' I said, as everything finally came into focus. 'You say…he was still alive in 1977?'

Sugden took a puff on his pipe and gave a nod. 'Aye. Reckon 'e was.'

Puff, puff. Like he had all the time in the world. Which I guess he did. *I*, on the other hand…

'Well, how do you know? Why didn't you tell anyone?'

'Realised after, din't I?' he said.

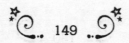

'After *what?*'

'After t' picture were printed. In t' paper, like. Bolton Abbey Easter Fayre. He were doing a sheepshearing demonstration. I thought, blow me if that int Archie Booth.' Another puff on his pipe. 'I'd covered that story, see, over an' over: about his disappearance. Got to know his family an' that. Only this feller had a different name, didn't he? Martin Busbys.'

'So what made you think he was really Archie Booth?'

'Somethin' about him,' said Sugden. 'Oh I know he'd have been thirty-six by then, and we only had pictures from when he were twenty-one, but...he'd not changed much. Filled out a bit. I tried looking up Martin Busbys in the phone book, but there were no listing. Editor sent me back to Bolton Abbey, thought this could be a big story. But no one there had heard of Martin Busbys. I even made a list o' nearby farms. Asked around a few of 'em. Nothing. Eventually my editor said, "You're wasting your time." Not enough to go on. So I had to give up.'

'And that's it?'

'That's it.'

'So...you don't actually *know* that Archie Booth was still alive in 1977,' I said.

'Nope.' He puffed on his pipe.

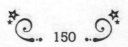

'But I thought you said—'

'Listen, I've given you what I've got, you can make what you like of it,' said Sugden. 'But you can stop wi' all the hollerin' after him, won't get you anywhere.'

Great, I thought. I've taken the risk of going AWOL with Kamal and crossing to the other side – which quite literally *scares me half to death* – for this?

'Right, well…thanks,' I said, trying not to sound too annoyed. I turned to Lupa. 'OK, good job, brilliant, we're done here – now get me the hell back to the land of the living, please!'

'Kitty? Kitty!'

Kamal's face was hovering over me.

'Oh! Right!' I stood up – then my legs buckled under me.

'Kitty!'

'I'm OK, really; I'm…just give me a minute.' I sat and waited for the pins and needles to subside – for my spirit and body to finish melting together.

'I am never doing that again!' said Kamal. His face was yellow.

'Me neither!'

'I kept checking the time,' said Kamal. 'It felt like *hours*. And you were so…so…'

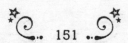

'Dead-looking?'

Kamal nodded. 'I know you told me not to freak out, but…the stuff that was running through my mind. I couldn't help thinking what if–'

'I'm sorry, Kamal,' I said, finally managing to stand up; I felt a lot stronger now. 'I shouldn't have put you through that – but I really appreciate it.'

'And your phone was going off…'

'Oh, hell.' I got my phone out: voicemails from Maro.

Message one:

'I'm in the laundry room…where are you, Kitaki-mou?'

Message two:

'Kitty, these clothes didn't come out very clean…did you forget the washing powder? I'm doing them again. Where are you? Come back now, please.'

'Argh…ten minutes ago.' I called her straight back. 'Heeeyyy, I'm sorry! I ran into Kamal and we lost track of time…yeah, the signal went…sorry! I'm coming back now.'

The date at the head of the yellowed old newspaper was 14 April 1977.

Well, hey, it was worth a try.

I'd told Sam and Floss all about my encounter with

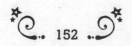

Sugden and, first chance we got, we went back to the library newspaper archives. Didn't take too much searching through the big purple-bound volume marked '1977', since I knew I was looking for a story about an *Easter* fair.

I turned over the pages, not daring to get my hopes up. Really, what were the chances that Lupa's version of things was at all reliable? Then I reached the centre spread, where there were lots of pictures and the headline read:

BOLTON ABBEY EASTER FAYRE

The pictures showed small kids on an Easter egg hunt, smiling ladies showing off their prize cakes…and then *boom*, there he was: the sheepshearer.

'Oh my God, this is the shot, look: Martin Busbys!' I gasped.

'Wow,' said Flossie. 'Hey, I see what the guy meant; it *does* look a bit like him.'

'Yeah,' agreed Sam, 'even though he'd have been, what, thirty-something by then?'

'Thirty-six,' I said. I'd printed out the picture of Archie at age twenty-one; I put it next to the sheepshearer one. 'Well, he looks older, obviously – and

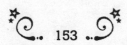

heavier. It doesn't help that he's looking away from the camera–'

'That's probably deliberate,' said Sam.

'Yeah, I guess…what do you think, Floss?'

Flossie frowned. 'OK, I'm confused. I thought you said Archie wasn't clever enough to change his identity and all that?'

'Yeah, but that was before…' I trailed off. I had to admit, it didn't seem very likely. What on earth would make us think this was anything other than just some guy that looked a bit like an older version of Archie Booth? 'Well, Mr Sugden thought it looked like him,' I said lamely.

'But *lots* of people look like each other,' said Flossie.

'Yeah, and how come no one found him, if he was right here in Yorkshire?' said Sam. 'There was a huge search for him.'

'I don't know,' I said.

'Maybe he *did* go far away, then came back years later, and by then everyone had forgotten all about him,' suggested Flossie.

'Hmm…it's possible.'

We all stared at the picture. We stared at it for a long time.

'OK, so he went missing fifty years ago, right?' I said at last.

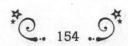

'Yeah.'

'Well, I'm just thinking...you know, round Bolton Abbey, that's right on the edge of the Yorkshire Dales, where there's, like, nothing for miles...'

'Except farms,' said Sam.

'The *occasional* farm in a great blodge of nothingness – and the whole area would've been even less populated back then. I wouldn't be surprised if some of the people were a bit out of touch, maybe hadn't even heard of Archie Booth – or at least never seen a picture of him.'

'I guess,' said Sam.

'But he'd changed his *name*,' said Flossie. 'You said he wasn't smart enough to do that.'

'No, I said he wasn't smart enough to change his *identity* – new look, new passport, that sort of thing... there's a big difference between all that and just giving a false name.'

'There's something weird about that name,' said Sam. 'Busbys. Who's called *Busbys*, with an "s" on the end? It's Busby, surely.'

'I was thinking that,' I said. Remembering something, I flipped back a couple of pages to a full-page ad for a spring sale. 'It's also the name of a department store... see?'

'Oh yeah...Busbys. Ha!'

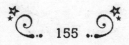

I flipped forward again to the sheepshearer picture, desperately searching for something else I might not have noticed before. Something looked not-quite-right about it, but I couldn't figure out what it was. 'OK, come on: what else can we tell about him from this picture?'

'He ate a lot,' said Flossie.

'He's whispering "mint sauce" in that sheep's ear,' said Sam. He and Flossie began to giggle.

'No, I've got it!' I said. 'He's left-handed!'

'Oh yeah,' said Flossie, peering at the way Martin Busbys held the electric shearer. 'So?'

'Archie was too!' I said. 'Mrs Booth said so. I remember now, she said he got teased for being "cack-handed".'

'Ew,' said Flossie. 'That means poo, doesn't it?'

Being left-handed myself, I'd come across the expression before. 'Yeah,' I said. 'We left-handers are disgusting, didn't you know? We wipe our bums with the same hand we eat with.'

'EEWW!' squealed Flossie.

'Never mind that,' said Sam. 'This is really interesting!'

'It is, isn't it?' I agreed.

'Is there anything else you can remember Mrs Booth mentioning, that could be relevant?'

I racked my brains to think of anything else. 'She

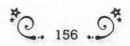

might have said other stuff here in the library,' I said. 'But to be honest I was kind of tuning her out, trying to do my work. Other than that…just, you know, on and on about what a good boy he was, how he was bullied, etc. Kids at school taunted him with cruel songs. That's about it. Oh, and how he was wrapped up warm, at least; guess she was trying to reassure herself that he wouldn't perish, like that woman on the moor did, back in March.'

'He had his donkey jacket,' said Sam.

'Yeah. And warm socks and DMs. So his little toesies wouldn't get froze.'

'Donkey jacket. DMs. Hmm…'

'Yes, well, not much use, is it?'

'Wait! Shh, I'm thinking,' said Sam. He shut his eyes tightly.

Flossie and I looked at each other, then back at Sam.

'DMs,' he said.

'Uh-huh.'

'As in Doc Martens.'

'Yes, of course…oh! Martin. Well, so what? "Martin" had a pair of Doc Martens. What a coincidence.'

'*Not* a coincidence,' said Sam. 'You know what, Kitty, I think it might be worth trying to track this guy down after all!'

I frowned at him. 'Why, because of the DMs?'

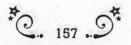

'That, plus "Busbys",' said Sam. 'What's the betting his coat came from that department store? That would explain the "s" on the end of his name, wouldn't it?'

'Oh! Well, I guess it *could…*'

'Yes, yes, think about it!' said Sam, all excited now. 'Just imagine: you're not the sharpest knife in the drawer, and you're wandering the countryside, homeless… you're looking for a place to stay, and some farm work. You find somewhere. They ask your name, and even though you're not too bright, you know enough not to give your real name. All your school days, your name was there, sewn into your uniform, written in your shoes. So it's logical, isn't it? First thing you'd think of. Martin, Busbys. Probably didn't occur to him to knock the "s" off the "Busbys".'

I felt a stupid grin begin to spread across my face. 'Sam! My God, that's brilliant! Ha! It's a wonder he didn't call himself "Doctor".' I nudged Flossie. 'Whaddaya think? I know he's a bighead, but Sam *can* be a bit clever sometimes, can't he?'

'Yeah,' said Flossie, vaguely.

'She's not convinced,' said Sam.

'No, it's just…I still don't understand how you're gonna find out where he lives,' said Flossie.

'Oh, right,' I said. 'Well, how hard can that be? There

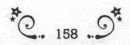

must be a phone listing or something.'

Back at the computer, we did a Google search: plenty of 'Martin Busby's, but no 'Martin Busbys'es. No phone listing. I typed into the search box, 'how to track down a missing person', but that was all stuff about looking for someone who'd only just gone missing.

'Type in "long-lost relative" instead,' suggested Sam. That was more helpful – until we found that there didn't seem to be any record of a Martin Busbys having got married or had kids – or having been born, for that matter.

He didn't exist.

We were about to admit defeat, when Flossie said, 'Why don't we ask the librarian for help?'

'What? You must be kidding,' I said. 'If she thought we'd tracked down a missing person, she'd probably get straight on to the police. If we really are on to something here, that might completely ruin Archie's life. Plus, I so don't want to get into *how* I know these things about him, or how we got involved in the first place.'

'Actually, you don't have to worry about any of that,' said Sam.

'Huh?'

'You're just looking for *Martin Busbys*. She wouldn't have any idea who he is, or any reason to connect his

name with the Archie Booth story. Just tell her the same thing you told the computer: you're looking for a long-lost relative.'

'Oh…yeah, that would do it, I guess. Maybe.'

'You just have to be really convincing,' said Sam. 'And win her over with your irresistible charm.'

'Ha! Well, she already thinks *I'm* off my rocker,' I said.

At this point, both Sam and I turned our gaze on to Flossie. Lovely, cute, butter-wouldn't-melt-in-the-mouth Flossie: perfect.

Martin Busbys

Riding my bike along the river-side trail, I thought to myself, *What on earth am I doing here?* All alone, heading out to some godforsaken middle-of-nowhere place I'd never been to before, way over the other side of a desolate moor. Hardacres Farm. And this time I didn't even have Lupa's help. I could have asked her, but…no: I wasn't *that* crazy. Besides, she wouldn't have a clue how to find this place; no ghosts involved.

But I had to go now; this was probably the only chance I'd get. Today was Friday; on Monday we'd be leaving for Scotland, and Saturday and Sunday were already completely crammed with visitors and stuff.

Sam wasn't happy. 'Let me come with you,' he'd said.

I nearly said yes, but changed my mind. 'You should go on to Kamal's, like we planned,' I told him. 'Just tell

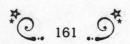

him I've got a headache or something. That way you'll be covering for me till I get back, 'cause Maro will think I'm with you. Anyway, I won't be gone long; it shouldn't take more than an hour. I'll be fine!'

Yes, I'll be fine, I told myself as I pedalled over the bridge across the river. It was no big deal! All the same, a shiver of nerves ran through me; I was now entering unknown territory. *You could just turn back*, said a voice inside my head. It was late: it had to be about twenty to eight by now. I could just give up; forget the whole thing.

No, that was ridiculous.

Ditch this now? And risk being haunted by Mrs Booth for the rest of my life? I didn't know whether she was capable of moving beyond her home zone, but I didn't fancy finding out the hard way. She was a powerful spirit, I knew that much: quite possibly Class A.

Of course, Mrs Booth wasn't my only reason for wanting to get to the bottom of this. In the whole two weeks since my first encounter with her, nothing – not even the help of an (admittedly bonkers) spirit guide – had led me to Archie Booth's ghost. I had to know whether this was because my phantorama was failing me, or because he was still alive. The phantorama was

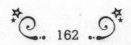

one thing I certainly *was* stuck with for the rest of my life; if there was a reason I might not always be able to connect with a dead person, I needed to know what that was.

I pedalled harder, reminding myself what a fantastic opportunity this was. Getting Flossie to work on that librarian, Barbara Hewlett: what a key move that had been! Turned out she had full access to this electoral register thingy, and guess what? Martin Busbys was on there. Not only that, he was *still* there, on the current year's register. How exciting was that? The same guy from the 1977 newspaper, still alive, still in Yorkshire! Seventy-one years old. 'I hope your granny enjoys meeting up with her long-lost cousin,' simpered Ms Hewlett, as she handed Flossie a slip of paper with the address on it. 'So lovely of you to surprise her like this!' Flossie batted her eyelashes.

I rode on.

Already it felt as if I were in the middle of nowhere, on a narrow country lane cutting through woods and fields. Here was a turning; I stopped to check my route. Maro had better not notice the map and compass were missing.

A niggling thought kept popping into my head. What if Martin Busbys turned out not to be Archie

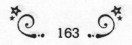

Booth at all? What if he were some *other* left-handed sheepshearing person, with a name that had nothing to do with Dr Martens boots or a donkey jacket from Busbys department store? What if I turned up, and asked him, and…what if? What if?

Oh, stop it with the what ifs! One thing was for sure: I wouldn't be summoning Mrs Booth just yet; if I'd got this wrong, there would be hell to pay.

OK, it wasn't this turning I had to take, but the next one. Pretty soon there'd be another turn on to a bridle path that would take me up to the moor. After that, it was practically a straight route all the way. 'Easy!' I said aloud, pretending not to notice the shake in my hands as I put the map away. I'd be there in twenty minutes, no trouble – and this time of the year, it didn't get dark until getting on for ten o'clock at night. I had loads of time.

An uphill stretch had me panting and sweating, until at last the road levelled out, and I came to what looked like the bridle path. *This has to be it*, I thought, as I unhooked the latch on the gate. I consulted the map again; well, if I was right, a reservoir would soon appear on my right. And yes, after a few moments, there it was. OK! I was getting pretty good at this navigation lark.

Then the cow fields gave way to wilderness. My, but this moor was deserted; not like Ilkley Moor at all. *Blubberhouses Moor.* How the hell did it get a name like that? Sounded like somewhere it never stopped raining, ever. Well, at least that wasn't the case right now: the high cloud was thinning out into golden evening streaks. I felt the warmth of the low sun behind me, giving me a long black shadow. Hey, at least I had my shadow for company.

The old man appeared in the doorway before I had a chance to check if I had the right farm. Old, *old* man: no way could this be our Archie. His scrawny hand clutched on to the collar of a black Labrador that was barking its head off. 'Can I help yer?' asked the man, eyeing me suspiciously.

I felt my face go hot. 'Oh, uh, I was looking for Hardacres Farm.'

'Yer looking at it,' said the man gruffly. 'I'm Hardacre. An' if this is about t' packin' work, yer too late: we found someone.'

'No, no, it's not that,' I said, stepping forward. 'I just…' I could hear my pulse pounding in my ears. *Out with it.* There was nothing else to do but just go ahead and say it. 'I'm looking for Martin Busbys,' I said. 'I've got a message for him.'

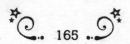

'Oh, aye,' said the old man. 'Well, anything yer've got to tell Martin, yer can tell me. I'll pass it on.'

Good. OK, so Martin Busbys was here. Not too soon to start homing in on Mrs Booth, then: I needed her here now. I hadn't dare summon her before – and even now there was some risk that Martin wasn't her Archie. But I felt I was so close now…

'Oh…well, it's kind of personal,' I said.

'Can't be so personal as I can't know about it,' snapped the old man. ''E's busy right now.'

I found myself wishing I had Flossie with me. She could melt the heart of even the stiffest old curmudgeon. I stepped closer. *What would Flossie do?* I tried out my best doe-eyed look. 'Please, mister,' I began. 'I know you don't know me, but I promise you, I have something very important to tell him in person, and it really can't wait.'

The old man folded his arms. 'Aye. And *I* told *you*, I'll give 'im t' message. What's it regarding?'

Huh, so much for the Flossie approach. Seemed I just didn't have the gift. 'Well…would you please just tell him it's to do with his mum?'

'His *mum?* Give over! He's not 'ad a mum around fer donkey's years.'

'No, well, what I mean is, his mum's *ghost.*'

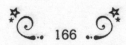

'His mum's…? Oh, don't be wastin' my time wi' all that nonsense,' said the old man, and he slammed the door in my face.

Oh brilliant. Now what? I stood there on the doorstep, helpless, watching a chicken scratch around in the yard. Glancing over at the smeary window, I saw a net curtain twitch. Then a pair of curtains was drawn.

I stepped down from the doorstep. No way was I going to give up this easily! I wandered slowly across the yard, thinking. Maybe a note? No, not a chance it would reach his hands. Without another moment's thought, I found myself making a semicircle round the side of the house. But it seemed the old geezer had thought of that one already; the back door burst open, and out rushed the black Labrador, *arf, arf*! I hurried back to my bike. Just as I was getting on it, I noticed the barking stopped abruptly. I glanced over my shoulder; the dog was eating something, and there was someone standing over it. A large man. He stepped closer. 'Psst!' He beckoned to me.

I hung on to my bike and walked over to him. He was chunkily built and tall but round-shouldered, and virtually bald, apart from a silvery stubble around the edges. He wore a pair of ancient corduroys and a plaid shirt with a vest poking out from under it. Could it be…?

'I 'eard what you said, about me mum,' he said. 'I'm Martin.'

Now that I was closer, I could get a good look at him. Right sort of age – about seventy – right build…eyes too close together. But it was impossible to say for sure if this was Archie Booth. Well, there was one way to find out. I couldn't put off contacting Mrs Booth any longer; this was a gamble I'd have to take.

'OK, good, thank you…just a minute,' I said, and I shut my eyes tight and concentrated all my thoughts on Mrs Booth. I called her out loud. 'Mrs Booth, I need you to join me, now!'

'Mrs Booth!' cried Martin. 'You called her Mrs Booth!'

I opened my eyes and saw his look of amazement. 'Yes,' I said.

The dog abruptly stopped snaffling around with its bone, looked up and whined. It had sensed a presence. Catching a flash of turquoise in the corner of my eye, I turned to look. 'Oh, and here she is now.'

Martin peered in the same direction. 'I…I don't see her.'

'No, you won't,' I said, propping my bike up against the wall. 'You won't hear her either. But she's there.'

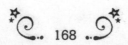

'Archie?' said Mrs Booth, stepping closer. 'Is that my Archie?'

The back door opened, and the old farmer appeared. 'What's going on?' he asked.

Martin held up his hand, as if to silence him.

'I think it is,' I told Mrs Booth.

'You think it is what?' asked the farmer.

'I think Martin's real name is Archie Booth,' I said.

With that, 'Martin' keeled over and collapsed.

Reunion

'I'm sorry, I'm sorry, I'm sorry,' I said, as Mr Hardacre and an old lady I took to be his wife bent over 'Martin', fanning him and attempting to revive him.

'What's up?' said another, younger man, who had just appeared. 'What happened to Martin?'

'Oh, Gareth, he's that badly shocked,' said Mrs Hardacre. 'He's out like a light!'

'I'll sort him out,' said Gareth, kneeling down and pulling him up into a seated position. 'Hey, Martin!' he said, giving him a gentle smack on the cheek.

'Huh…wha…?' said Martin/Archie, tugging on his left ear as his eyes began to focus.

'Oh, it *is* him!' gasped Mrs Booth, sinking to her knees in the dirt beside him. 'He always did that thing with his ear when he was anxious or confused… Archie, my boy, it's *me*, love! It's your mum!'

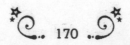

'Mum!' cried Archie. 'Mum, I can't see yer, but I can feel yer, I knows yer here. Oh, Mum!'

'Oh, Archie!' cried Mrs Booth.

'Oh, Mum!'

'By 'eck, what you on about, Martin?' asked Gareth.

Martin/Archie sat up and burst into tears, rubbing his eyes with his fists like a little kid; *deeply* weird to see an old man behave like that, I can tell you. 'Me mum!' he blubbed. 'She's here in spirit...*she* brought her; the girl!' He pointed to me.

'Now look 'ere,' said Mr Hardacre, turning to me. 'I don't know what your game is, but—'

'I'll deal with this, Dad,' said Gareth, getting up. 'Who are you?' he asked, as he came towards me.

'Oh...never mind about that.' I backed away, reaching for my bike. 'Look, I only came to reunite Archie with his mum, OK? She's been searching for so long—'

'*So* long!' wailed Mrs Booth.

'...And now that I've done that,' I added, 'I'll just—'

'Wait!' said Gareth, grabbing me by the arm.

I felt the panic rise to my throat. 'I told you, Mrs Booth just wanted to find her son!'

'Now you leave her alone, young man!' said Mrs Booth.

'He can't hear you,' I said.

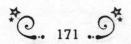

171

'Who can't?' said Gareth.

'I was talking to Mrs Booth,' I explained.

'You one o' them clairvoyants then, are you?'

'Um…yeah…'

'How old are you?'

'I'm…sixteen,' I lied.

'Oh aye?' said Gareth. 'And I'm the Pope's uncle. Bit of a troublemaker, aren't you? I've a mind to turn you in to the police.'

'No!' I cried, then felt like kicking myself. 'I mean… I don't care. It's just there's no point, is what I meant.'

Gareth smirked; he wasn't fooled.

Distracted by all the drama, I was a bit late to realise something. 'Hang on; I could report *you* to the police!' I said at last. 'Hiding Archie all these years!'

Archie interrupted his murmurings to protest, 'They never done nothin' wrong!'

'That's right,' said Mr Hardacre. 'Archie were a grown man when he came to us. So even if we'd known he'd run away from home–'

'Which we didn't,' said his wife.

'…Which we didn't, not for a long while,' said Mr Hardacre, 'weren't nowt against t' law anyhow.'

The ghost among us began wailing. 'Oh Archie, I'm so sorry…I'm so, so sorry!'

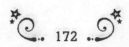

'Mrs Booth says she's sorry,' I told Archie.

'It weren't her fault!' cried Archie. 'None of it were her fault. But I couldn't abide it any longer…' He started blubbing all over again.

'Oh Martin…there, there,' said Mrs Hardacre. 'Come on; we'll go in and have us some tea.'

'I…I'll be off, then,' I said.

'Oh no, you won't,' said Mr Hardacre. 'We've words to have with you.'

Seeing as Gareth still had a strong grip on my arm, I didn't feel I was in much of a position to resist. 'Erm, OK.'

And then the whole story came out: how Archie had just cracked one day. Set out across the moor, as he often did when he was upset – only this time he'd kept right on walking. He didn't have a plan or anything: no money, no food. He'd just walked and walked, across Baildon, Bingley, Ilkley moors, drinking the spring water…spent a night sleeping rough. Then up through Blubberhouses Moor, into the Dales.

Finding a farm up there, he'd managed to get a bit of work, and a barn to sleep in. It was just as Sam had guessed: the first time someone asked his name, he'd just blurted out, 'Der-Martin…Busbys,' after the names inside his clothes. People always asked if he didn't mean

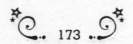

'Busby', and he always insisted that no: it was Busbys-with-an-s, but 'Der-Martin' straight away got shortened to just 'Martin'.

He'd drifted for two years, often sleeping rough, just getting by. Then he'd come to Hardacres, and stayed ever since. 'He never got a wage, as such,' Mrs Hardacre explained. 'Just pocket money, on top o' the free bed and board.' After the first year, Hardacre had wanted to put him on the payroll; it was then that Archie had explained, in his own way, that Martin Busbys didn't exist on paper – and why.

Hardacre remembered something from radio reports – they didn't have a television back then, and he said he didn't have time for newspapers. So they'd never seen the pictures. Archie talked about his years of torment, of never feeling he belonged – not even at home. That was the part of the story the newspapers hadn't found out about: his father had beaten him. And when Archie grew big and strong enough to retaliate, he was terrified of his own rage: he'd thought he might kill him.

I looked at the gentle giant child-man Archie with his red, dripping nose and sad eyes. I thought of all the terrible pain and heartache he'd gone through, and suddenly I was furious. I turned on Mrs Booth. 'Your husband beat him – and you didn't stop him? Aren't you

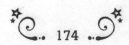

ashamed of yourself?' I leapt to my feet. 'My God, who do you think you are, lecturing *me* about bullying?' I demanded, becoming even more shrill. 'I'm not surprised poor Archie ran away!'

'I loved my husband!' Mrs Booth snapped back. 'It was just his *way*. He thought he'd make a man of him.'

'What'd she say?' asked Mrs Hardacre.

'It was "just his way",' I said. 'Ugh! What a hypocrite!'

''E didn't do it to the others,' said Archie, who'd begun rocking rhythmically, his arms folded. 'Only me.'

'Aw, pet,' said Mrs Hardacre, patting him on the knee. She turned to me. 'Don't be so hard on his mum, dear. I do believe she loved him very, very much.' Her eyes were glassy with tears.

'Then she should have protected him!'

'You don't understand. Things were different back then.'

'She's right,' said Gareth. 'His dad...I'm not making any excuses for him, but there wasn't the understanding of people like Martin – Archie – in them days, not like there is now.'

'Aye, an' it were men still ruled the roost,' added Mrs Hardacre. 'Women didn't get half the say in things as they do now.'

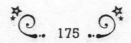

'Damn right, an' all,' muttered Hardacre.

Mrs Hardacre ignored him. 'Don't judge her, love, is all I'm saying.'

'She were good to me, she were,' said Archie.

I sighed. 'Well…I've got to go.'

Gareth jumped up. 'Just a moment. You're not to tell anyone about…about who Martin really is.'

'She's not to breathe a *word*,' warned Mr Hardacre, his eyes throwing me those poisonous darts of his.

Mrs Hardacre tried a gentler, more persuasive approach. 'Martin's happy here, love,' she said. 'All that publicity…he wouldn't be able to cope. You do understand, don't you? There's no harm in it.'

'No harm in it,' echoed Archie, shaking his head vigorously while he went on rocking.

'Oh, I'm so glad he's happy!' said Mrs Booth. 'You will tell him that, won't you, before you go? I don't expect you ever to understand how it was, but just…just do that one thing for me, will you? And I'll be away myself, for good.'

Now I was getting all teary too. I stepped forward. 'Archie – Martin – your mum says…' I cleared the lump in my throat. 'She says…she's glad you're happy.'

'*Thank you*,' said Mrs Booth. 'I'll be on my way now. Goodbye, Archie; I love you.'

And with that, she shone brightly for a moment, her headscarf fluttering in some ethereal wind, and then she was gone.

There was silence. The dog went over to where Mrs Booth had been, and sniffed.

Archie looked at me. 'She's gone, ent she?'

'Aye,' I said. 'I mean, *yes*. She wants you to know…she loves you.'

Archie's voice was croaky with emotion. 'Thank you, er…what's your name?'

At that moment, the clock on the mantelpiece chimed: nine o'clock.

'Oh my God, I've got to go!' I gasped, lunging for the door. 'I won't tell anyone you're here, Archie; I promise. I don't care, it's fine, whatever…I understand. But I've got to go!' I dashed out, through the hall and the kitchen to the back door. I leapt on my bike, and rode away. As I went, I could hear Gareth calling from the front door, 'Stop! I'll give you a ride!' but I didn't hesitate, just kept on going.

The Barghest

I'll be fine, I told myself. Twilight was setting in, but I'd be fine: still enough light to see by. The only part I had to worry about was the first bit, crossing the moor, and I knew the way now. I'd easily do it in twenty minutes – less, even. Once I was on the road I didn't even need to worry about it getting dark.

My head was buzzing with it all, as I cycled on to the path that crossed the moor. My God, Archie was still alive, after all! And I'd actually met him! I couldn't wait to tell the others. How brilliant were we? We'd actually tracked him down, fifty years after he'd disappeared. What a team! OK, so we weren't going to tell anybody else – I'd make sure of that. But I also felt a little thrill at having reunited him with his mum. It had meant closure for them both; they'd forgiven each other. It felt good: gave me a warm glow inside.

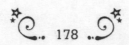

I wondered what was going on back at the campsite. Well, I hadn't heard from Maro yet; that was good. Sam was doing an effective job of covering for me. But I was going to be late back; I'd better call and warn him, or he'd be worried. I was on the part of the moor that was an uphill climb; arriving at the top, I stopped and reached into my pocket for my phone.

It wasn't there.

Then I remembered; I'd left the Hippo in such a hurry, I'd forgotten to bring it. Now I really was going to have to hurry. What if Sam called me, and Maro picked it up, and...? I just had to not think about it; I whizzed down the hill as fast as I could. I'd soon be back.

The sky was completely clear now: deep blue like a bottomless well. One brilliant star, one moon. Either full or almost full: I never could tell. But beautiful. Good: more light to see by. Once again, not a human soul on the moor except me, but I wasn't afraid; at least I had the sheep for company. Although, to be honest, they creeped me out a bit. I didn't like the way they stared. At least the grouse were being quiet; probably asleep.

And now: water. There was water, burbling nearby. I slowed down; the path crossed a rocky stream.

No! This wasn't right: there hadn't been a stream before!

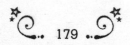

I felt a hot, prickling sensation all over. I must have taken a wrong turn somehow…maybe back at the top of the hill? My breath shortened as I pulled out the map. Oh no… It wasn't easy to see in this light, but it looked as if there had been a fork in the path up there; I hadn't noticed it. Coming in this direction, things looked different – plus, I'd been distracted. So much for my knowing the way.

OK.

Deep breath.

This wasn't so bad. I'd just cycle back up to the top of the hill, and…and just to make sure I was getting back on to the right path, I'd use the compass; I needed to be heading almost exactly due south, then south-west-ish. I felt in my other pocket for the compass. Oh my God. I didn't have that, either. I checked the bag I was using for the map and my water bottle…nope. I knew I hadn't put it in there anyway; it had definitely been in my pocket. Must have fallen out… Fail.

Never mind. I would cope with this. I was sure I knew where I'd gone wrong, and I still had the map. *Yeah, and much longer and you won't even be able to read it,* said an unwelcome voice in my head. Well, I would just take a left when I got to the crossing; that was bound to be the right way. Onwards and upwards.

A faint, distant howl echoed across the desolate hills.

Arooo!

It sounded like... No, don't even think it.

It *wasn't* the killer dog. The killer dog didn't exist. It was just some sheepdog somewhere.

It wasn't that other thing, either – the phantom dog, the Barghest. No. Such. Thing. Complete fiction.

Because if either of them existed, where were all the corpses? Archie, I now knew, was still alive. Probably Neil Hatch was, too; it would explain why I'd failed over and over again to reach his spirit – even with a spirit guide. The only corpse so far had been the woman who'd died back in March, and there was nothing to suggest she'd been savaged by a wild dog. It *could* have been a fright that made her fall, but...no. There was no killer dog, no Barghest; they were just myths. Besides: those myths were connected to *Ilkley* Moor, not Blubberhouses—

Aroooo!

'Omigod!' I squeaked out loud. It was nearer this time. And the moon was...oh right: that moon was just one big gorgeous silver platter. A perfect, awful circle... perfect for *werewolves*. No, no: they didn't exist!

Get to the top of the hill, take a left, I told myself. You'll soon be out of here. And stop being paranoid.

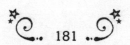

Now it really was getting dark. Damn! What was the matter with me? Why hadn't I let that Gareth give me a ride home? *Because you don't get into vehicles with strangers, dumb-ass.* And you'd thought you'd be on the other side of the moor well before nine thirty, and now it was…hell, I didn't even have any way of checking. Not that I wanted to.

Aroooo!

Oh God, oh God, oh God…I love you, Maro. I love you, Sam, I love you, Flossie, and I'm sorry: I'm so, so sorry…

The crossing! Here it was, at last. Yes! Yes! I could be off the moor in, what? Ten minutes? I'd be *fine* now! I'd be OK! Only…oh no. This wasn't the turning, after all. But it was somewhere around here, I was sure. I would concentrate on searching for it, and *not* think about the dog, or the Barghest…

No, don't think about it!

Killer dog.

Stop it!

Barghest.

Arooooooo!

I stopped breathing. It was right there. I could hear its footsteps…I could hear its hollow, gravelly breath…

And then, right in front of me: two gleaming eyes.

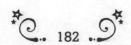

20

Sanctuary

It was standing right in my path. Big, dark, hulking great creature, the breeze ruffling its fur. Silvery muzzle, glistening black nose, gleaming amber eyes pinning me to the spot. Oh yes: it was a *wolf*, all right. This was not some pet dog intimidating strangers, like they sometimes do.

It was just me, and a wolf.

Out on the moor.

At night.

Not a soul anywhere else for miles, as far as I could tell. And I didn't even have my phone. Not that that would have been much use: *Hey, can someone come rescue me? I'm out on the moor, and there's this wolf that's about to eat me. I'm on one of the paths, round about the middle-ish bit...*

Right. As if.

I didn't move. Maybe if I just stayed *really still*, it would think I was a statue or something. Yeah, a statue. One that inexplicably smelled like a *tasty human being*. A *scared* human being. Because animals could smell fear, couldn't they?

I could back away, I thought. Trouble was, that would have meant getting off the bike, and *that* would have meant movement. Better to just, like, not move. I wished I could die on the spot: just expire all by myself, there and then, and save the wolf the trouble of actually killing me. It felt as if that might just happen anyway, as I waited for the pounce, which would surely come any second now...

Only it didn't. The wolf just stood there, fixing me with that stare, not even growling or anything. And then, the most unbelievable thing happened. It gave a little whine, then started panting and wagging its tail. When it came up to me I flinched a bit, but I didn't freak out at all, because what was absolutely crystal clear was that it was being friendly.

And then I knew.

'It's you, isn't it?' I said. 'You're Lupa.'

At that point, the wolf reared up on its hind legs, laid its – *her* – paws on my shoulders and started licking my face. Her icy tongue chilled me to the bone and her

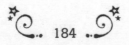

breath smelled like rotten dead things, but I was ecstatic. All the tension in my body relaxed, and I began laughing hysterically. 'Oh Lupa,' I cried at last, 'have you come to get me out of this mess?'

Back down on all fours, she wagged her tail harder, repeatedly glancing in the direction of the path ahead and back at me, as if to tell me yes, that was exactly what she was going to do.

'Wow,' I said. 'I never thought I'd be so glad to see you. OK, girl: let's go.'

Well, I got away with it – just.

As we reached the entrance to the campsite, I got down off my bike, petted Lupa's icy coat and thanked her. Her face was full of doggy happiness as she stretched it up to mine. I half expected her to change back into her human form at this point, but she didn't; instead, she just turned and trotted away.

'Oh!' I cried. I didn't want her to go. I felt a lump rise in my throat once again, as I watched her silvery tail disappear into the night.

'Kitty!' said Kamal. 'You OK?'

I'd rushed over to his caravan as fast as I could. 'Yeah, I'm good!' My voice came out all strangulated,

and my face felt hard and tight like frozen chicken. 'Is everything…are they…?'

Sam and Floss appeared. Flossie looked like she was about to burst into tears. 'God, you're OK!' said Sam. 'How'd it go?'

'Good, really good,' I said.

They all stepped outside; Kamal pulled the door to so it was almost closed. 'You mean you found Archie?' he whispered.

We hadn't told him about our Martin Busbys discovery, and I certainly wasn't about to give anything away about that now. 'Yes,' I said. 'I found his spirit. He and his mum are reunited now. Listen, we've got to get back to the Hippo now – but thanks, Kamal. You've been a great help – really.'

Kamal shrugged. 'It's OK.'

We said goodbye and hurried home.

'Jeez, Kitty, I was *this* close to calling Maro,' said Sam.

'Yeah, we were getting really worried,' said Flossie.

'I know, I'm sorry…'

We returned to a darkened Hippo. 'You are *so* lucky,' said Sam. 'Maro must still be over at the Hippiemobile.'

I felt like I was about to burst; finally I could blurt out the whole story about what had happened up at

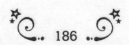

Hardacres Farm – and on the way back. It all came out in a jumble, and I had to go over everything a second time, filling in bits I'd missed out the first time around. 'Now remember, you're not to breathe a word about Archie to anyone, OK? Not Maro, not Kamal – no one.'

'Maro wouldn't tell anyone,' said Flossie.

'Yeah, but…all right, maybe – one day. Not now. But honestly, he wouldn't be able to cope with all the attention in the papers, the telly…and the Hardacres are really old.'

'Yeah, it's OK, don't worry,' said Sam. 'Wow: amazing, isn't it? Mystery solved!'

'Yeah…' I said, scratching my head. 'Still none the wiser about Neil Hatch, though.'

'Yeah,' said Flossie. 'Plus there's those other people who might've been killed as well.'

'Come on Floss, that cover-up theory is just dumb,' I said.

'Yeah, but can you *prove* it's not true?' she asked.

'No, but–'

'You can't prove a negative,' said Sam. 'It's like with aliens in outer space: just because we haven't *seen* them, doesn't mean they're not there. In fact, statistically–'

'Yeah, but what if someone got found out over

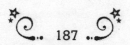

a cover-up?' said Flossie. 'That would be proof, wouldn't it?'

'Ye-es. But–'

'Or what if Jim was caught going out on to the moor and getting his dog to maul people to death?'

'Right,' said Sam. 'Well, looks like you've got your work cut out for you, if you're going to figure all that out. And you've got just two days left, before we leave.'

'OK, never mind all that,' I said, 'I'm going to concentrate on Neil Hatch. I'm convinced now that he's still alive. That bird sanctuary: we haven't been there yet. We should go.'

'Yeah!' said Sam. 'Don't worry, Kit, the birds there won't attack you: they'll all be in cages.'

I thwacked him.

'Ow!'

'How is going to the bird sanctuary going to help?' asked Flossie.

'God knows. But…you got any other suggestions? I dunno, maybe there's stuff we can find out about him there.'

'Stuff the police haven't found out already?' said Sam.

I thrust my face towards his, all goggle-eyed. 'But *I* have special POWERS, Sam,' I said in a phoney magician voice, with hand gestures to match.

The door opened, and Maro came in. '*Pethakia*! Bed!'

'Yeah, sorry.' I was relieved to see that she apparently suspected nothing. 'Hey, Maro? Could we go to that bird sanctuary place?'

Maro put her arm around me and said in a stage whisper, 'Ah, you want to use your phantorama to help find this missing guy, right?'

'No, I just…'

'Well, if it helps at all,' Maro said, 'Brian knows this woman Robyn who runs it.'

'Ha! Robyn!' said Sam. '*Bird* sanctuary…*Robyn*.'

I rolled my eyes. 'Yeah, we get it, Sam.'

Flossie laughed. 'What's her last name? Pigeon? Hawk? Raven?'

Raven. Of course. Suddenly, I knew exactly what I wanted to do…

21

Eggs

I sat with my face wedged against the bus window, craning my neck: yes, there it was! The raven, flying alongside us. At least, it *looked* like the raven.

Crazy idea...so many layers of crazy! Never mind how the hell I was going to ask it to help me find Neil Hatch; what on earth made me think it *could* help, anyway? But Maro says sometimes you just have to trust your intuition: you find yourself doing things that don't make much sense at first, even to you, but there's a signal in your brain, telling you to do it anyway.

So, hey: I had a go.

I had no way of summoning it, so I'd just gone down to the stream the next day and waited.

When it had finally appeared – landing once again on a branch right at eye-level – I stared at it. It stared back.

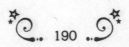

I wasn't creeped out by it any more – I just felt stupid. It was a *bird*, for heaven's sake! One hell of a clever bird, yes, but still a bird. How was I going to communicate with it? In raven-speak?

Well, I muddled my way through. Lots of stupid talk and gestures, like some English people do when speaking to foreigners, and shoving a newspaper picture of Neil Hatch under its beak. Yup: mad. I couldn't tell whether it had understood anything. It seemed to nod.

But now, a day later, here it was! So I guessed, at the very least, it had understood the 'follow me' part. And here it was again, as we headed through the gate to the sanctuary: perched on the fence, head cocked to one side, eye gleaming.

'Watch out, Kitty, it's another one of those creepy black birds, out to get you!' said Sam.

I just smiled knowingly. It was *my* raven, for sure.

Then it flew off. It was gone for some time. We trailed around the place, looking at the owls, the eagles…all the time I was wondering if anything else was going to happen.

We passed a chunky blond woman in overalls, carrying buckets; I recognised her as Neil Hatch's boss from the TV report.

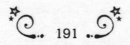

'Oh hi, are you Robyn?' said Maro. She introduced us, saying we knew Brian.

Robyn paused, but didn't put down the buckets. 'Oh, hello,' she said, awkwardly. 'Well, er... Sorry, I'm a bit rushed at the minute. But I'll be back at the Visitor Centre in about half an hour...'

'Oh, I am *so sorry,*' said Maro melodramatically. 'You must be short-staffed; forgive me. I saw in the news about–'

Robyn grimaced. 'Neil: yes. That's bad enough, but now I've got someone else off sick – been nearly a week. Well, I hope you're enjoying your visit.'

'Yes, you have so many beautiful birds here,' said Maro. 'And I like that grassy roof of yours,' she added, gesturing in the direction of the Visitor Centre.

'Our "green roof", yes,' said Robyn. 'Lovely, isn't it? Full of wild flowers this time of year. Heavens, just listen to the racket those birds are making! Well, I'll be back in a while.'

The birds certainly were making a racket. And they all seemed to be gathering just above the Visitor Centre, swooping and darting this way and that, and cawing and chippering and squawking. Something was going on.

Robyn left, and Maro started reading off some info about an injured falcon we were looking at.

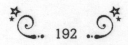

The noise above the Visitor Centre grew louder. I looked up: even more of them now. Crows, starlings, pigeons…even some grouse, I reckoned. Something was definitely going on up there.

'I'll, uh…be back in a bit, OK?'

Maro gave me an exaggerated wink. 'OK, *Kitaki-mou.*'

I hurried back to the Visitor Centre, and after a moment or two the birds flew off in different directions, leaving just one behind: my raven. It was perched on the roof. 'Ark!' it cried, then swooped down to me. Then off it went again, back to the same point up on the roof. It cawed again, and repeated the whole action. It was trying to draw my attention to something, up there on the roof.

I ran after Robyn, and eventually found her cleaning out one of the cages. 'Robyn…that green roof…on the Visitor Centre?' I gasped.

Robyn blinked at me slowly, like an owl. 'Yes?'

'Erm…' What to say? *My friend the raven is summoning me to it?* Right.

'I'm sorry, this is going to seem really weird, but…could I go up there?'

*

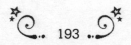

A sudden feeling of dread filled me as I began to climb the ladder. What if the thing that the raven was drawing my attention to was Neil Hatch's dead body? The thought hadn't actually crossed my mind until now.

Argh. Served me right for going up without Robyn's permission, I supposed. She'd looked at me like I was a loony: said she didn't have time for this sort of thing, I'd have to explain exactly why I wanted to go up there, etc., etc...

It hadn't taken me long to find the storeroom. Unlocked! No doubt thanks to Robyn being overworked and understaffed. Plus, thankfully, it was just round the back of the Visitor Centre, so I didn't have far to drag the ladder. But now...now, gruesome images of rotting corpses were filling my head. *No, it's not possible!* I told myself. If there'd been a body up there, it would have been found by now. People would have noticed birds pecking at it, and God knows what. *There is no body, Kitty.*

So...what would I find?

I forced myself to climb the rest of the way. I looked around, and heaved a sigh of relief. No corpses. None that I could see, anyway; the grass was quite long, and peppered with daisies, cornflowers and buttercups. The raven flapped down and settled in a spot some way

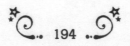

up and to the left of me; it cawed again, jerked its head up and down. I clambered up, gripping on to tufts of grass as I went. And there, half hidden by the grasses and covered in bird poo, was a small skylight. The raven tugged at a blue nylon webbed strap that poked out from the top of it, then let go. I pulled the strap, and the window swung open.

'Hey! What's going on!' called a voice: Robyn. I slunk in through the window: no way was I giving up on this now! Thud. I dropped to the dusty, bare-boarded floor. There was nothing in the tiny room – no, it wasn't even a room; there was no door. The tiny *space*. Nothing in there except piles of box files, like you see in offices, only stacked on their sides.

'Get down from there *now*, do you hear?' came Robyn's distant voice.

'Caw!' cried the raven back.

'That's right, you tell 'er,' I said. 'What *have* we got here?' I opened one of the box files. It had been divided into sections that were stuffed with cotton wool. Nestled in the cotton wool were eggs: not normal chicken's eggs, but little speckled ones. I opened up some more boxes: every single one was filled in the same way. Blue eggs, beige eggs, dark, black-spattered eggs…eggs that looked like those Cadbury's ones.

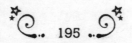

'Caw!' the raven cried again; it flapped away. Then Robyn's face appeared in the skylight. 'What on earth...?'

'I'm sorry! I know I shouldn't have, it's just...I didn't know how to explain, but I...I think this might be important.'

Robyn clambered in, all red-faced and sweaty from the exertion. She picked up the open boxes one after another and gazed at their contents, her face full of wonder. 'You're damn right it's important! Woodcock, partridge, wood pigeon, grouse...' She looked up and gasped. 'God, I can't believe it! So this is what he was up to!'

'What? Who?'

'Neil...it could only be Neil. This is *why*, don't you see? My God, I have no idea how you discovered this, but...this is incredible!'

'I don't understand!'

By now, Sam and Floss had evidently discovered what was going on and now they appeared at the skylight too.

'OK, sorry, sorry,' said Robyn, wiping the sweat from her face with her sleeve. 'Let me explain: this...this –' she held up two box files, one after the other – 'threatens the survival of bird species, and is illegal. It all makes

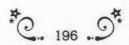

196

sense now – this would be why Neil was getting death threats. There are some conservationists who feel very strongly about this indeed, and… Oh no. I've just realised something else.'

'What?'

Robyn gulped hard. 'The death threats. I think I know who's been sending them.'

22

Witches

After that, a lot of stuff happened very fast – and then nothing happened for ages.

Robyn got straight on to the police, and made everyone leave. She'd explained that the person she suspected was another employee of hers – the one who'd been off sick for a week. She was now thinking the guy wasn't really ill at all.

For most of the rest of the day, there was no news. We were just waiting, waiting…

'How *did* you find that egg collection, Kit?' asked Sam, on the ride back.

I described what had happened – though I was careful when talking about the raven in front of Maro, and avoided letting on about anything Archie Booth-related.

'What? You're honestly saying that all those other birds *told the raven* about it?' said Sam.

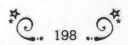

I gave him a withering look. 'We're not the only species that communicates, you know, Sam.'

'Yes, but…they were all different species of bird, weren't they?' said Maro. 'Does a raven know how to communicate with a pigeon or a, a…*ena helithoni*? Whatever: other kinds of bird.'

'I guess they must have found a way,' I said. 'Must have been a hell of a lot of birds that were *really upset* over losing their eggs.'

'Hmm…I suppose there could be some sort of inter-species network,' said Maro.

'Yeah,' said Sam, frowning and nodding in mock-seriousness. 'I guess there must. Wow, I wonder what they call that. Twitter?'

I gave him a sharp poke. 'Oi! This was an important discovery, you know! I don't care what you believe; we've just moved this investigation into a totally new direction.'

'Yeah, all right, fair enough.'

'If anything, you'd think the birds would have ganged up on Neil Hatch and attacked him,' said Flossie.

'Yeah, right, Floss,' I laughed. 'I think that's the sort of thing that only happens in movies.'

'OK, so how come no one else ever found this egg collection, that's what I'd like to know,' said Sam. 'How come the police never looked up there?'

'Why would they?' I said. 'They were looking for a *missing person*. Nobody knew he was an egg collector. He was obviously very good at keeping it a secret – which he'd have had to do, because it's illegal.'

'No, it isn't, it's unlawful,' said Sam.

Maro frowned. 'What's the difference?'

'Well, see, unlawful is against the law–'

'…And an ill eagle is a sick bird,' I added. 'Yes, thank you, Sam.'

'A sick bird!' shrieked Maro. She howled with laughter, then proceeded to tell her neighbour the joke, and laugh really loudly all over again.

Sam and I rolled our eyes at each other. 'Well done,' I said.

'Sorry.'

'Anyway, you're right, I'm sure the police would have searched the building for clues. But they'd have gone to all the *accessible* parts. I don't know if you noticed, but that part seemed to be completely sealed off.'

'OK, yeah…that place was the size of a cupboard. I guess there must've been a proper room up there at one point, or why else would there be a window?'

'Well it's definitely closed off now,' I said. 'No door

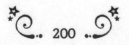

or anything. The police wouldn't even have spotted the skylight from outside, because of the green roof. *They* didn't have a bird's-eye view of things.'

That evening we watched the news, but there was no mention of Neil Hatch – not even about the discovery of the egg collection.

'Well, they wouldn't make that public, not yet,' said Sam. 'Not if they're trying to track down this guy who made the death threats.'

'Argh, I don't want to leave for Scotland tomorrow morning,' I said. 'I wanna know what happens!'

'Oh, Kitty, it'll be on the news if they find him,' said Maro. 'Anyway, if it makes any difference, I've been thinking of staying for an extra day anyway; Cathy wants us to stick around for the summer solstice.'

'The summer what?' said Flossie.

'The longest day of the year,' said Sam.

'Oh. Why should we hang around for that?'

'Because there's quite a ceremony up at the Twelve Apostles stone circle, apparently: a pagan ritual. Cathy wants to check it out, and wants us to go with her.'

'Oh, like they do at Stonehenge?' I said.

'Kind of like that, yes,' said Maro. 'So will you come?'

I thought about the last time I was up at the Twelve

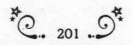

Apostles: all those moaning spirits. I didn't much fancy it. But then, that had been before I'd sorted out Mrs Booth; *she'd* been the one who'd whipped up that whole frenzy, I was sure of it – and she wasn't around any more. Plus, it would mean getting to stay an extra day.

'OK,' I said.

The sun was setting, and the distant moorland was dark purple beneath the brilliant orange strip of sky, and the pink-tinged clouds. Now we were miles from anywhere, cut off from the news, which we'd been checking on the radio every hour since we'd got back from the bird sanctuary. Cathy was with us, plus a whole gang of other people we'd never met. Most were chatting among themselves, but one or two were curious about us, in a friendly way. Most were dressed in normal casual clothing, but one or two wore hooded cloaks, and several had on long white robes, and floral crowns on their heads.

'Why are they dressed like angels?' asked Flossie.

'I don't know,' said Cathy. 'But I don't think they're meant to be angels, Flossie; it's just about being at one with nature, I suppose. There'll be a service and everything – it's a proper religion for these people. But

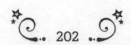

not with formal choirs, or anything like that. Oh, where is Ben? He's taking ages!'

'What's he up to?' asked Maro.

Cathy groaned. 'Oh, helping Brian out with something – *again*. That's Ben for you; doesn't sit still for a minute. They've been gone all afternoon.' Then she added cheerfully, 'Oh well, either he comes or he doesn't; I've got you for company!'

It was a gorgeous evening – and the pagan service was kind of interesting in a weird way. By the time we'd settled down at the Twelve Apostles and the whole thing had got going, I actually found myself almost forgetting the whole Neil Hatch business. This was *so* not like any kind of religious service I'd ever been to, it wasn't funny – or rather, it *was* funny.

There was this thing where we all had to stand facing the north and wave our arms about and pray to the north wind. Then we had to do the same for the south wind, the east wind and the west wind, and I had to try not to giggle, because it was meant to be serious but I just felt like I was five years old again, doing music and movement in reception class. Any minute now we'd be doing sleeping lions.

Then we sat down again, a circle of people sitting cross-legged within the circle of stones (which, I was glad

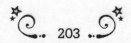

203

to see, were behaving themselves, and not doing the moany-groany thing like last time), our faces lit by dozens of flickering tea lights out there on the bleak, black moor. It was pretty magical, actually. People began taking it in turns to recite poems or sing or play music; some of them were *terrible*, but one or two were not bad, actually.

As a woman was singing, a dark figure with a flashing torch approached: Ben. 'Heeeyy!' whispered Cathy once he'd reached us; she reached up and put her arms around him. 'You made it! Where's your guitar?'

A space was made in the circle for him next to her; he sat down. 'Haven't got it,' he whispered back. He seemed tense.

'Oh! But...'

Ben squeezed her arm. 'Sshh... Tell you later. Don't worry, it's all good...it's all good.'

The song came to an end, and there was light applause.

Someone else stood up, and began playing the flute. After a moment or two, some woman started moaning along to it. At first I thought we were in for more really rubbish singing, and I braced myself for another stifled giggle. The moaning seemed to be coming from one of the hooded figures. Then all of a sudden, she cried out: 'Aargh!'

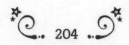

The flautist stopped dead; several of us got up. Sam and I flashed alarmed looks at each other, and the first thought that entered my head was, *Oh my God, we're witnessing a murder!*

But she didn't slump forward with a dagger in her back.

Instead, she fell sideways, into the arms of her neighbour, and her hood went askew; for the first time we saw her face.

'Kaylee!' cried Maro.

Yup: Kaylee. Maro and Cathy rushed to her side, along with several others. 'Oh, I'm sorry!' cried Kaylee, clutching her big, round belly that had previously been hidden under the cloak. 'I'm so embarrassed! But I think...I think the baby's coming!'

'It's not due yet though, right?' said someone.

'Not for another two weeks,' said Kaylee. 'But... aargh!'

'Oh now, don't worry,' said Maro. 'We'll get you comfortable...if it is coming, you've got several hours yet, at least.'

'She's right,' said a woman with a garland of daisies round her neck. 'Took me *forty-eight* hours with mine! Don't you worry, Kaylee; I'll bring my car round in a while. Just relax – tension just makes it worse. Breee-eathe.'

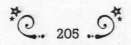

Kaylee did as she was told, taking long, deep breaths. She turned to Maro. 'You won't tell my parents, will you?'

Maro blinked at her huge belly. 'Well, Kaylee, I don't think–'

'I mean, about me being here,' said Kaylee. 'They…they wouldn't understand.'

'Oh! Well, of course…'

'They *really* wouldn't understand,' said the daisy woman. 'As in, they think we're witches.'

'Which we are!' said another woman, cheerfully.

'*Witch* we are,' said a man, to a ripple of chuckles.

'Yes, I know some of you are,' said Kaylee, 'and very good ones, too!' She turned to Maro and Cathy. 'That remedy for high blood pressure…only thing that worked for me…OW!' She shut her eyes tightly and bared her teeth like a vampire, then threw her head back and howled in agony.

That's it, I thought. *I'm never having a baby.*

'That's another contraction already?' said Maro, who Knows About These Things. She looked at her watch. 'That's very close together! OK, *kamari-mou,* let's get you to the hospital.'

'Oh…oh!' wailed Kaylee. 'But I can't walk! And the car's, like…way down by–'

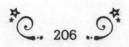

206

'Don't worry,' said another man, who was holding a mobile phone. 'I've just called an ambulance. They can drive on the path nearly all the way, then use a stretcher.'

Kaylee's face was flushed; she closed her eyes like she was praying. 'Thank you,' she breathed. 'Oh, please hurry, please hurry…'

Meanwhile, the rest of us were standing about like lemons. I had about a million questions I wanted to ask Kaylee, but it didn't exactly feel like a good moment.

Then she calmed down for a bit, and said to Maro, 'No, really…you won't tell me mum and dad, will you?'

'No, of course not,' said Maro; Cathy agreed.

'Thank you,' gasped Kaylee. 'I've tried explaining that it's my religion, but they just don't get it; they're convinced it's wicked. They even stopped me meeting the group at the pub. So then I took to goin' out later, after they were asleep.'

I felt my ears prick up like a dog's, as I remembered the time I'd seen their car leaving late at night, freewheeling down the hill. 'Oh! Uh…really? Like, in the car?'

Kaylee frowned. 'Well, yeah.'

Wow: well, this explained a lot. All the same, they were living in a *caravan*: the people you share it with

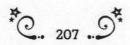

207

know what you're up to, pretty much the whole time. I should know.

'And…they never heard you?'

'Car's parked on a hill, see?' said Kaylee. 'I just take the brake off and let it go, till I'm far enough away. Plus me dad snores like a foghorn anyway. And the dog…the dog…argh!'

Again, she writhed and screamed in agony. When the contraction was over, she just managed to explain that her witch friend had supplied a very good, completely harmless herbal sleep potion, which she'd been feeding to Carlos the Rottweiler each night so he wouldn't be disturbed. The downside was that he slept so soundly, he was up at the crack of dawn each morning, bursting with energy. 'And then I have to listen to ten minutes of swearing, while me dad gets ready to take him for a walk,' said Kaylee. She managed a faint smile. 'But it's worth it!'

Then came a different scream: the faint sound of an ambulance siren.

As Kaylee was helped into the ambulance, Maro offered to go with her. 'Aw, thanks Maro!' said Kaylee. 'But it's OK; got me mates here, haven't I?' Miss Daisy and another young woman were with her; they nodded.

Then they piled into the ambulance, and it drove off.

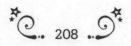

'Oh, *stin evlogia tou Theou*, I do hope it all goes OK!' said Maro.

'She'll be fine,' said Cathy. 'She's in good health. Even if she gives birth in the ambulance, they'll know what to do. What I want to know is what's been going on with you, Ben!' she added, turning to her husband.

'Oh, Cathy, I'm sorry I couldn't tell you anything before, but…I got roped into helping out on this police search, here on the moor – but I wasn't allowed to say anything. Brian asked me; he was able to help them locate the most likely spots where they might find that missing guy – Neil Hatch? But they needed all the help they could get, as it was time-sensitive. And…' Ben gave a big sigh of relief. 'He's been found.'

'Alive?'

'Yes, alive – but if we'd left it much longer he might not have been. He came very close to being hunted down…'

'Oh my God – by the other guy at the bird sanctuary?' I said.

'How did you know?'

'We were there yesterday,' said Maro. 'There was some egg collection, or something?'

'Exactly,' said Ben. 'Seems the guy was secretly collecting eggs from all the birds of the moor. They

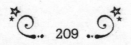

worked out he was missing just one: a late breeder, and a bit of a rarity – the merlin. That guy who'd been sending the death threats, he'd figured all that out too–'

'The one who'd taken time off work,' I said.

'That's the one,' said Ben. 'And it seems he was intent on carrying out his threat. They got him too.'

'Oh, thank God for that!' said Maro.

'Well done, Ben!' said Cathy, throwing her arms around him.

'Oh, it wasn't me,' said Ben. 'There were several teams of us out there. It's incredible, you know: that egg collection was well hidden, apparently. Whoever found it did so just in time, it seems!'

The House of Tomorrow

So. Archie Booth: check.

Neil Hatch: check.

And if you believed the police line about the woman back in March (and there was really no reason not to) then there was no mystery surrounding that, either. Which just left…the sheep.

'So I guess this murderous dog only eats sheep,' said Flossie next morning over breakfast.

'Uh-uh.' Maro shook her head vigorously, mouth full of toast, chewed, then swallowed. 'There is no murderous dog, *Flosaki-mou*. These people like Jim who spread that story just made the whole thing up about the sheep.'

'How d'you know?'

'All right, let's just say it's most unlikely, *pethaki-mou*,' said Maro. 'Brian knows a lot of people around here,

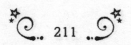

211

including sheep farmers; he doesn't know anyone who's lost any sheep in suspicious circumstances.'

'So there *could* still be a monster out there…' said Flossie. Now that we were leaving, I could swear she seemed almost disappointed that there might *not* be one.

'*Most unlikely*,' said Maro. She yawned and stretched. 'Oh, *The-eh mou*, I am tired after all that excitement last night! Let's leave tomorrow, huh?'

I smiled. 'You really just want to see Kaylee's baby, don't you?'

'Well, that too,' admitted Maro. She gazed out of the window. 'Anyway, it's a nice day; Cathy and Ben have invited us along for a picnic at…Woodland Crag, or something. It's a bit of a walk, but that's OK, my ankle's better now.'

Great idea. Only what Maro hadn't realised was that it wasn't *Woodland* Crag we were going to, but *Woodhouse* Crag – the location of the Swastika Stone.

As we approached it, her face turned white. She clung to me and whispered, 'I'm keeping a close eye on you, *Kitaki-mou*.'

'Maro, d'you think I *want* to get yanked through that portal?' *Again*, I didn't say. 'If it really is a portal, that is,' I added. 'Probably isn't.'

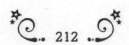

Maro narrowed her eyes at me. 'Hmm...I'm not taking any chances.'

Thinking about the portal got me wondering about Lupa again. I hadn't seen her since four nights ago, and then only in wolf form. Was that it, now? Was she gone for good?

We settled down for our picnic on the slope just above the path that led to the Swastika Stone, with the whole of Ilkley laid out before us. Some other friends of Cathy and Ben's had come along too: the kids were really young – pre-schoolers. As I sat watching them frolic around, I noticed another figure appear beside them: Lupa. She was acting like she was part of their game, darting this way and that like an overgrown toddler – though of course the kids were oblivious.

'Lupa!' I called softly.

She looked up and waved, then came skipping over. 'Hello, friend!'

I stood up. 'Where've you been?'

'Sleeping!' said Lupa.

'*Sleeping?*' For one thing, it had never occurred to me that ghosts slept at all – and for another, it had been four days. 'It's been four days!' I said.

Lupa shrugged. 'Really? Hey, you find Martin Busbys yet?'

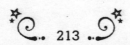

'You…you don't know? Oh, I guess not.' I realised I hadn't actually said anything to her when she was in wolf form about what had happened up at Hardacres Farm, because…well, because she was a wolf. I gazed around. Spotting a nearby tree, I pointed to it and said to Maro, 'I'm just going over there for a minute, OK?' I needed something to hide behind, so people wouldn't think I was a complete nutter, talking to myself.

'*Se parakolou tho*,' she said, which means 'I'm watching you' – only she said it with a big grin and a nod, as if she was saying, 'OK, that's cool', or something.

I went over to the tree, and Lupa followed me, skipping. 'Kitty, I dream about you!' she said. 'When I'm sleeping. I remember now. It's night-time, middle of the moor, and you're lost. I find you and I take you home!'

'Lupa, that was no dream,' I said. 'That really happened – four nights ago. But you were…you were in one of your other incarnations. A wolf.'

'Oh!' said Lupa.

'So…I guess you stayed that way a while.'

Lupa nodded. 'I suppose so. But feels like a dream.'

'Anyway, yes, I found Martin Busbys; thank you.' I told her the whole story of my visit to Hardacres Farm, how 'Martin Busbys' really was Archie Booth, just as Mr Sugden had thought, and how I'd brought Mrs Booth's

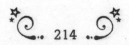

spirit to her son, so she could now be at peace, and move on. 'But…as you know, I got lost on the way back. So thank you for helping me there, as well.'

Lupa beamed at me. 'So now you make me pretty?'

'Erm…' What on earth was I supposed to do? I felt like saying, *Give up: that face ain't fixable! Be a wolf instead: you make a* gorgeous *wolf!* Only I didn't, of course. Instead, I just said, 'Lupa, I think "natural" suits you best. Just be yourself.'

She did that thin-lipped pout of hers, then glanced over at the Swastika Stone. 'Well, no matter. I finish here. My seven days are up, so I must return to the other side now.'

'Oh…OK.' I didn't like to mention it had been *way more* than seven days. I found myself wishing I could see my lovely Lupa wolf again, just one more time. Or even that she could stay like that, and be a sort of guardian to me, my ghostly wolf companion…

'Do you have to go?' I asked.

'Yes,' said Lupa. 'Only then can I be reborn. And I do something to help you; this means my next life be a good one.' She held up her hand. 'Goodbye, spirit sister!'

We touched palms. Then she turned and skipped down to the Swastika Stone. I watched from a safe distance as she felt about for the portal. I saw the four-armed crank appear and begin spinning, faster and faster: she dived into it, and was gone.

We headed back to the campsite, through Heber's Ghyll, a rocky stream that led through woodland. The little kids were still totally hyper: shouting, laughing, tripping over, crying, laughing again.

Sam, Floss and I followed behind, and I told them what had happened with Lupa.

'So she's gone for good, huh?' said Sam.

'Yup.'

'So that's…a good thing, I guess.'

'Yeah, I s'pose.'

'You *did* say she was really annoying,' said Flossie.

'Yes.'

I sighed. It was a lonely business, having phantorama. No one else really understood what it was like. You'd make connections with spirits – but then they never stuck around. 'Well, hey, but this is our life now, isn't it?' I said. 'We move on. Always, we move on…'

Suddenly, the little kids fell silent, and one of them said, 'Eeurgh!'

'Dare you to pick it up,' said the other.

We caught up. 'What is it?' I asked.

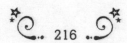

The kids pointed.

'Oh!' I cried, clamping my hand to my mouth as I gazed down at the small feathered black corpse, lying on its side, that one jet pearl eye, now lifeless, staring back up at me. I knew right away; it was my raven.

The kids' mother came over, warning them not to touch it.

'What happened to it?' asked the little boy.

'It's gone to heaven,' said his mum.

'Couldn't it of flied there?'

'No, only its soul can do that. The body has to stay behind. Come along, now.' She took his hand and led him away.

I stood there for a moment, gazing at the raven. Had all that effort been too much for it? Or was it like Lupa: done with its work? Maybe it had atoned for its sins, and it was time to move on. I hoped its next life would be a good one.

WEDNESDAY 22 JUNE

Your children are not your children.
They are the sons and daughters of Life's longing
for itself.

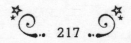

I have now learned the whole thing off by heart. Well, hey, it's a long drive up to Scotland. And it's now officially my Fave Poem. What REALLY blows my mind is this bit:

You may house their bodies but not their souls,

For their souls dwell in the house of tomorrow,

which you cannot visit, not even in your dreams.

It makes me think of Archie Booth, whose dad completely didn't understand him.

It makes me think of Kaylee's lovely, healthy baby boy. He arrived when HE felt like it, thank you very much, right there in the ambulance on the way to the hospital. So glad we got to see him before we left.

And it makes me think of Lupa: what will be *her* house of tomorrow, I wonder? I mean, for all we know, she might already be reincarnated. Hey, she might even be…OMG!

OK, I just asked Maro about this, i.e. when does a baby get its soul – before or after it's born? And she says, definitely before – but she has no idea how LONG before. 'People have been debating that for a very long time,' she says. Ah well…who can tell, anyway?

I'm thinking maybe none of Lupa's previous lives can have lasted very long. She's so childish – if anything, it's like she's the opposite of an ancient spirit. I hope for her that the next life will be longer; maybe she's earned that now.

No clues from Kaylee's baby's appearance. He looks just like any other newborn: dark peach fuzz on his head, navy blue eyes, tight little pink fists. Well, I hope he gets by OK. Let's face it, it's not a brilliant start: they don't seem to have much money…there's the horrible, scary grandfather…and no dad around, apparently. But he seems to have an ace mum. That's got to count for something, hasn't it?

And maybe – just maybe – he's come into the world knowing stuff that'll help him get on in life – go 'swift and far', like in the poem. He might turn out be a top footballer, like Kaylee was joking about. Or a brain surgeon. Or a poet. And he'll think, *Hey, I don't know how come I'm so good at this, but…go me!* And that'll be his House of Tomorrow.

Oh: Kamal gave me a genie!

Well, he gave me a pretty little box. It's red velvet with gold piping on it. And he says that any time I'm REALLY STUCK with my phantorama, I can open up the box and imagine that my genie floats out and hovers there smiling, ready to help me out. OK, so it's only a pretend genie, but it's the thought that counts.

Like he said, it's what you believe that matters.

Glossary of Maro-isms

Oh, po po, ti messi mou [o po-**poh**, tee **mess**-ee
   moo]...... Oh, my aching back!

O Jimmis [o **Jim**-iss]......Jimmy (literally, 'the Jimmy'!)

to bobo tou [to bo-**boh** too]......his backside

piyenoume [pee-yen-oo-may]......let's go

O Theos kseri [o **thay**-oss ksair-ee]......God knows

stin evlogia tou Theou [steen ev-lo-**hee**-ah too **Thay**-
   oo]......God bless her

Se parakolou tho [say pa-ra-ka-**loo** tho]......I'm
   watching you

ena helithoni [enn-ah hel-ee-**tho**-nee]......a swallow

Acknowledgements

Thanks as ever to Maria Street for all the help with the Greek expressions – any inaccuracies are down to me, not her! Thanks to Sally Nicholls for her help with one particular piece of research – it was fun! Thanks also to the helpful staff at Ilkley Library, and to Alison at the Census Office. And thanks to my brother Stuart and sis-in-law Jo-Anne for putting up with me while in Yorkshire. X

Don't miss the stunning series from
Holly Webb, bestselling author of ROSE

Magic will always find a way...

978 1 40831 349 7 £5.99 PB
978 1 40831 640 5 £5.99 eBook

978 1 40831 350 3 £5.99 PB
978 1 40831 641 2 £5.99 eBook

978 1 40831 351 0 £5.99 PB
978 1 40831 642 9 eBook

ORCHARD BOOKS
www.orchardbooks.co.uk